# A Cowboy for June

# A *Cowboy for June*

**A Three Sisters Ranch Romance**

# Jamie K. Schmidt

TULE
PUBLISHING

A Cowboy for June
Copyright© 2021 Jamie K. Schmidt
Tule Publishing First Printing, September 2021

The Tule Publishing, Inc.

First Publication by Tule Publishing 2021

Cover design by Llewellen Designs

ISBN: 978-1-954894-82-2

# Chapter One

JUNE GRAYSON WAS so happy to be on her horse, Athena, that she had to concentrate on the beautiful Texas scenery to keep from crying. She was half afraid that if she started bawling her eyes out, she'd never stop.

"You okay?" Emily Sullivan asked.

Emily was her ride-or-die BFF. June knew she had to be careful with her answer because if Emily caught even a whiff of bullshit, she wouldn't let up until June's carefully duct-taped emotions burst free.

"I will be," June settled on, guiding Athena down the new trails that the Three Sisters Ranch had built for Emily's fiancé's hunting lodge. "It's good to be riding again after being cooped up inside for so long."

Rehab had been a rude awakening and June had vowed to do everything in her power to make sure she never went back there. If that meant giving up on whiskey shots and tequila sunrises, it was worth it to not have to spend three more months of her life in a place that was part-hospital and part-prison.

At her last rodeo event, the shit had hit the fan. June didn't remember a lot of what she'd done just before she'd blacked out, but she'd woken up in a jail cell. After a depressing talk with the judge and a few attorneys, it had been decided that if June did a mandatory stint in a rehab center, all charges against her would be dropped. She'd walked in there a Women's Professional Rodeo Circuit All-Around Champion, and last week, she'd walked out unemployed, with the polite suggestion that she retire from the circuit.

Retire?

She was twenty-six years old. June had been barrel racing all over the United States and abroad since she was ten. What the hell else was she going to do with her life? Not so deep down, June was hoping the WPRC would change their minds about her, once her sister, Merry, buried Shayna and won the championships out from under her. She wasn't ready to give up that delusion just yet.

"Donovan better get back here," June said to divert Emily's attention. "I see feral hog tracks."

Donovan Link was Emily's fiancé. He and Emily had met when he'd rented some property on the Three Sisters Ranch, so he could host hunting parties. Then he fell in love with Emily, a die-hard vegetarian and animal rights activist. They compromised. The hunting parties were now only for population control. The rest of the time, he did nature safaris. Still, the feral hog problem gave him a steady amount of work. They were invasive, dangerous, and downright mean.

Emily made a face. "They deserve to live just as much as other wildlife."

June hid a smile. Emily was also taking over managing

her family's cattle ranch from her father, who really needed to retire. The irony of it, though, was delicious. They raised cattle for slaughter, and Emily wouldn't eat a steak if you held a gun to her head.

"Sure." June nodded. "But letting them overbreed and starve is just cruel."

"Go to hell," Emily said, without any heat in her voice.

June snickered. Too bad Emily hadn't risen to the bait. June had been looking for a good-natured argument, or at least a passionate debate about barbecue pork ribs. Maybe it would've gotten rid of the restlessness that was making her itch like a bad poison ivy spread. June and Emily had been friends since they were children. They had excelled in pushing the boundaries and their parents' patience with their weekly capers.

"How's April?" Emily asked. "Kelly's been moping around ever since April finished up Trent's taxes and went on to the next client."

April was one of June's older sisters, who was the same age as Emily's sister, Kelly. April was a CPA and had been making the rounds of all the Last Stand businesses, doing their taxes and other financial stuff that June couldn't care less about.

"She's doing good. I'm going to see her on Sunday when she comes over for dinner at Mama's."

"Is Cole going to be there too?"

"Probably." June rolled her eyes. "They're attached at the hip." April had found true love a little over three months ago. They were already engaged, and June was trying to keep her pessimism to herself.

Three months?

It would take three years before June would think a man was worth keeping, and then only if he didn't blow it in the meantime. She didn't have anything against Cole. He seemed like a good guy and was crazy about April. It was just that June and her sisters had seen what quick relationships did to their mother, Penny. All three of them had different fathers and none of the men in their mother's life ever stuck around for very long. Their fathers had cycled in and out of their lives—mostly just long enough to break their mama's heart again before leaving.

Cole, at least, had good references. He worked here, at the Three Sisters Ranch, helping Trent Campbell—a former rodeo star—teach kids how to ride bulls. Like Donovan, Trent had also rented property and wound up marrying a Sullivan sister—Emily's older sister, Kelly. Maybe June could ask him if he needed help training the kids on how to barrel race at his bull-riding school. Of course, Trent might not want to hire her, considering her reputation.

"How's it feel to be back in Last Stand?" Emily asked.

"Like I never left, especially since I'm staying in my old room in Mama's trailer."

"I bet she's happy to see you."

"She is. And it's good to see her, too. I just wish it was temporary while I waited for the next rodeo."

"I bet they'll change their minds and let you compete again. Just give it a few months."

June shook her head. "I doubt it. They don't want my

element messing up their family values."

"Everyone makes mistakes," Emily said stubbornly.

"Yeah, but everyone doesn't get into a fight with Shayna James." Rodeo princess and two-faced bitch, Shayna was all down-home sweetness for the cameras, but used a hot stick to prod her horse to go faster. Six thousand volts of electricity was a hell of a motivator.

"I can't believe she tried to claim that the cattle prod was yours."

That had been Shayna's first mistake. It had put Shayna on June's other sister, Merry's, radar. Merry didn't care who it was, she'd go after anyone who messed with her family. And she'd go full out. No hair pulling or scratching. Merry would use that cattle prod on Shayna if she got a chance. June might be powerless, but her sister wasn't. It was something.

"Well, you're the only one," June said. She would never put a spur on Athena, let alone zap her into going faster. And anyone who had ever seen her with her horse should have known better.

But June and Merry weren't well liked on the rodeo circuit. They didn't kiss ass. They didn't do the mean girl shit, and they certainly didn't cheat. But they weren't perfect little rodeo queens, either. She and Merry liked to party, and other people liked to gossip about that. Maybe they would have been better liked if they didn't win as much as they did.

June loved the attention though, good or bad. The fans, at least, appreciated the Grayson sisters. June had never wanted to be a role model for younger girls, but she and

Merry were always flooded after the events for autographs and pictures. It had been nice to have that type of validation. June even wore a black hat with the words *Bad Reputation* in sparkles around the brim. Unfortunately, you start to speak your fate into existence by doing things like that.

"Did you really cut her ponytail off with a switchblade?" Emily asked.

"That's what they say," June said. That was one of a few instances that June couldn't recall.

What she *did* remember was catching Shayna with her hand down Dustin's pants. And she remembered screaming at Dustin for cheating on her, and for his lousy taste in choosing Shayna to screw around with. Then June remembered polishing off half a bottle of Jack Daniel's, as she got angrier and angrier. And the last thing she remembered was doing an obscene mechanical bull ride for a bunch of cheering rednecks at a bar. Things got fuzzier after that.

At one point, June must have caught up with the happy couple again. Her knuckles had been busted open and Dustin had a broken nose. June had a vague memory of being sprawled out in the hay and mud, and Shayna kicking her in the stomach and ribs. Then there was nothing.

"You're lucky no one caught the action on their phone."

June nodded. She had half expected it to be all over the internet with memes and videos. But that hadn't happened. "I guess Shayna has friends in high places. That video would have ruined her image." June had gone searching for it once the rehab center let her have her phone back. The only thing she had found was Dustin and Shayna's engagement photos on Instagram.

Barf.

Shayna looked like a Karen with short hair. Dustin looked sexy as hell. Damn him. He must have got his nose set right away because there wasn't even a bump to show for the fistfight.

It had been his dumb idea to become exclusive. June had resisted doing that for so long, because she knew how men were. She'd had a ringside seat while growing up for the fiasco that was her mother's love life. Penny had become a chameleon, changing to fit whatever man she was with. She went through a homemaker phase, and one as a sex kitten. One month Mama was a rock groupie, and the next she had traded in all her concert T-shirts for conservative blouses and had become a church lady. It was enough to give a girl whiplash.

There was no way in hell June was going to put herself through that. She had been happily ignored to do whatever she wanted during her childhood and she was determined to keep it that way.

But Dustin had been persistent. And hot. Against her better judgment—and a lot of begging—he had worn her down. Finally, she'd agreed that they would be exclusive with each other. To be honest, it had almost been a relief not to wonder who she was going home with. Two weeks later, though, he was getting a handy from Shayna James in her horse's stall.

"At least Merry kicked her ass in the championships."

"Shayna's lucky that's all Merry did." June had been unable to take or make phone calls or have any contact with the outside world for a month after she had been forced by Sinclair Thompson, the head of public relations at the WPRC, to check into rehab. She had been terrified Merry was going to take revenge and wind up in a jail cell.

"So what are you going to do with yourself?" Emily asked the question that had been haunting June ever since she'd come back to Last Stand.

"I guess I've got to get a real job."

"Doing what?"

June shrugged. "I'm computer illiterate. I'm not cut out for customer service, though. Maybe I'll open up a brothel. I think I'd make a good madam. What do you think?" June waggled her eyebrows at Emily.

"I think that's illegal in Texas."

"I suppose I could go to Nevada."

"Do you have the money to start a new business?"

"Jeez Louise, you've been hanging around with April too much. No. I've got enough to last me a few months and then I'm going to beg the manager at the H-E-B to put me in the stockroom."

"You wouldn't last the week," Emily said.

"You don't know that." But June agreed with her. This was a depressing subject, so she changed it. "Are you ready for your bachelorette party?"

"I am, now that you're here."

"Do you have any idea where we're going to take you?" June asked.

"No, but I'm pretty sure that wherever we go, there's going to be a lot of shots involved. Are you going to be okay with that? You can tell my sisters, and they can make other arrangements."

Keeping away from the booze wouldn't be an issue.

"I'm not an alcoholic." June fixed an evil eye on Emily's expression, looking for disbelief or pity. "Even Linda, my counselor at rehab, said so. I honestly don't want to drink anymore. The thought of it turns my stomach." She swallowed hard. "I can't tell you how scared I was not to remember everything I did. I could have hurt someone. I probably did hurt someone, but they deserved it. And I got beat up. I think Shayna was responsible for my cracked ribs." They still twinged. June rubbed them absently. "I'm not going to make myself a target again. No cold beer after a long day is worth that. I'm keeping to seltzer water for now."

"How's that working for you?" Emily asked.

"It gives me the burps something fierce."

"Can you burp the alphabet?"

"Is that a new party trick of yours?" June asked.

"I'm just being silly because the conversation is taking a serious turn. You'd tell me if you had a problem, right?"

June scoffed. "I'm a big girl. I can handle being at a party where there's drinking. I can even have a shot if I want to. I don't want to."

"Why?" Emily asked.

"I liked drinking because I liked how out of control I felt. It was like being on one of our capers. But that last time..." June shook her head. "I've never felt that way before. I drank a lot, don't get me wrong. It was like everything ramped up in a hurry."

Emily frowned. "Are you sure someone didn't slip you something?"

The thought left June cold and she rubbed her shoulders. "I don't know." She had wondered that herself in the long months she was in the facility. No one seemed to believe that it could have happened, so she'd put it out of her mind. Shaking off the gloomy feeling, she said, "If I do decide to have a drink, it's not like I'm going to get blackout drunk again. That was a onetime only affair, as far as I'm concerned. Don't worry about anything but having a good time. And of course, doing shots off of the stripper's taut six-pack abs."

"How exactly does one do shots off of a man's abs?" Emily asked.

They both tilted their heads and thought about it for a minute or so.

"I think the stripper would have to be lying down," June said.

"That's so not happening. Do you want me to be divorced even before I get married?"

"It's a bachelorette party," June reasoned. "These things happen. What do you think the guys are going to be doing?"

"They're going to be playing poker."

"Strip poker?" June asked, rubbing her hands together.

"I really doubt it, and it's guys only. No women allowed."

They reached the end of the trail, so they circled their horses around and headed back to the ranch.

"I'm bummed that Merry can't make it back for the party. I haven't seen her since before I went into rehab. And with her schedule, it looks like I'm not going to see her until Thanksgiving."

"No," Emily said. "She promised me that she'll be at the wedding at the end of the month."

June didn't want to burst Emily's bubble, but she didn't think Merry was going to be able to make it. Of course, Merry was crazy enough to take a red-eye flight for a couple hours just to go to a wedding and then take another red-eye flight back, and still be ready to compete later that day. But June didn't want Emily to concern herself with anything but having fun. If it hadn't been for Emily's letters, and eventually her weekly phone calls while June was in rehab, June would have gone absolutely crazy. Emily had promised when she got out, that they would go on capers again, just like they'd done when they were younger. June had a few in mind, but with Emily being so busy with the ranch and planning for her wedding, they hadn't had a chance yet. Yet. June hid a grin at what she had planned for drumming up excitement for Emily's bachelorette party.

Every woman in Last Stand was invited. Emily's sisters had rented the back of Callum's Country Party House and sent out pretty invitations. Callum's was a fun date night spot, but tame. People went there with the expectation of playing games and having a few drinks. It had the potential to be an unforgettable night, though. Especially if June got people in the mood for a raucous time. Booze or no booze, she was champing at the bit. She wasn't used to spending time in one place, doing quiet things. Sometimes she wondered if the most exciting years of her life were behind her, now that she was out of the rodeo. The idea of being bored for the next sixty-odd years was terrifying.

"Do you think Shayna and Dustin check out my social media pages?" June asked.

"Why do you care?"

"I don't."

Emily snorted.

"Okay, so I want them to boil and writhe with jealousy at what a fantastic time I'm having. Especially since the last three months have been such a drudge."

"I think no news is good news," Emily said. "Let them wonder what you're up to."

"Hmmm," June said. But her mind was still on revenge. It wasn't healthy and she should probably talk about it with Linda. "I would also like to get on Sinclair Thompson's nerves."

"I don't think that'll help get you invited back to the WPRC."

"He goes out of his way to protect Shayna. I bet she's his secret love child or something."

"Maybe she's sleeping with him?" Emily said.

"Gross." June shuddered.

"You need to move on."

"I need to get even with them first. Merry will make sure Shayna is number two. But Dustin and Sinclair need to suffer too. You need to help me with this."

"As long as we don't get arrested," Emily said, sighing in

resignation.

"When have we ever gotten caught?"

"We were a lot younger then and there weren't cell phone and security cameras everywhere."

That was true.

"But I'll think about it." Emily gave her a conspiratorial smirk.

As they rode along the back trails, June really appreciated the fresh air and the sounds of nature. After spending most of February, March and April locked up in a soulless gray facility, it was absolutely liberating to feel the sun on her face while she and Athena moved like one unit. It had been hard not to be on horseback for three months, and while she probably was going to be sore tomorrow morning, June didn't care.

"Can't you give me even a little hint about the bachelorette party this weekend?" Emily said.

"Well, doing shots off strippers is now out. Thanks a bunch."

"You could still do shots off the strippers' abs. You don't have a fiancé wondering what the hell you're doing."

"Shots of what?" June asked. "No alcohol, remember?"

Emily grimaced. "Yeah, I suck. I totally didn't think. But hey, it's a bar. They've got mixers. Do a shot of orange juice or shot of club soda or something."

"Why don't I just snort some hot tea while I'm at it? I feel like a grandma."

"Don't let my mother hear you say that. She can't wait." Sarah Sullivan was already a grandmother. Kelly's daughter

Alissa was growing like a weed and Kelly had another bun in the oven and was about to pop. At least June wouldn't be alone in not drinking.

"Does that mean your mother's going to do shots off of the stripper's butt?" June asked, trying to picture it.

"Now it's off their butt?"

"You're the one who had a problem with abs."

"I had a problem with putting my mouth near a naked body that wasn't my fiancé's."

"Or maybe you and your mom are prudes."

"Let's face it, if anyone is doing a shot off a stripper's butt, it's your mom."

"That's pretty much a given." Merry and June were known as the wild Grayson sisters in the rodeo circuit. But they got that title from the original wild Grayson—their mother, Penny.

Mama was a hairdresser in town at the Clippety-Do-Da salon. And she was thrilled that June was home for good. She offered to share her tips with her if she shampooed and conditioned her clients' hair and swept up afterward. Mama thought June would be a big draw for the local women.

June thought having to explain the same things over and over again to every customer who came to gawk at her would drive her nuts in no time.

"I hope a lot of people come to my party," Emily said in a small voice. "I wanted the whole town to celebrate. It's been a tough couple of years for everyone."

"Don't worry," June replied. "I've got a surefire plan for that and you're going to help me."

"Great. It's not like I don't have a thousand things to do today."

"I just need you to be my getaway driver."

"Oh, June." Emily shook her head.

"That's not a no."

# Chapter Two

ESTEBAN LOPEZ WONDERED what normal people did on their days off. After working long damn hours at the Three Sisters Ranch, the last place he wanted to be was in the bunkhouse or trapped in his room. So he went over to his mother's house. She always saved up a week's worth of chores for him to help her with. But he truly didn't mind. After all, ever since his worthless father had left when he and his twin sister were twelve and the younger set of twins were four, Esteban had been the man of the house. He hadn't minded that, either. It gave him a chance to boss around his two younger brothers, Sam and Luis.

"Have you got jobs for your brothers yet?" his mom asked him, even before he got through the door.

"Not yet, Mamá. Soon," he said, taking the list she handed him. "The upstairs faucet is leaking again?"

"*Sí.*" She looked him up and down. "Have you been eating? You look sick."

"I'm fine. Just a little tired."

"You need a wife to take care of you."

Esteban looked at his watch. That had to have been a record. Less than five minutes. "I'm waiting for the right woman." He got his toolbox out of the closet and headed upstairs, with his mom following right behind him.

"What about Paloma, from church?"

Esteban bit back a grimace. Paloma had made it very clear that dating a ranch hand wasn't in line with the style of living she wanted to become accustomed to. "We didn't hit it off," he said, squatting down to get a good luck at the pipes under the bathroom sink.

"Carmela?"

Carmela didn't care that he was a ranch hand. She cared that he swore, drank, and gambled. Not to excess and certainly not in her presence, that he could recall. But it hadn't mattered. After their first date, she had called him back in tears and said she couldn't go out with someone like him unless he changed his evil ways.

"We didn't hit it off," Esteban said, lying on his back so he could better wedge himself into a position where he could caulk the leaking pipe.

His mother slapped her hands to her sides. "You're too picky. But I've found the perfect woman for you."

*Again.* Esteban's mind filled in.

"She's a good Catholic girl. She sings in the choir. She's smart. She's pretty."

"What's wrong with her?" Esteban muttered.

"What? I can't hear you. Don't mumble."

"What's her name?" he said in a clearer voice.

"Sofia Martinez. She's perfect for you. She wants to settle down right away and have a family."

Esteban's heart thumped. He didn't mind his mother's

matchmaking so much because he was ready to get married. He wanted kids and someone to come home to, instead of bunking with at least four other men every night. He thought he had found someone, but that was a long time ago. Valerie had wanted out of Last Stand, more than she'd wanted him. Esteban supposed it was for the best, but it still didn't stop him from wondering what would have happened if he had quit the Three Sisters Ranch and gone with her to Dallas.

"There is one teensy little thing, though."

*Here it comes.*

"She just got a job in Galveston, so it would be a long-distance relationship. Unless, of course, you decided to move there with her."

"That's rushing things a bit." Esteban had already patched up the faucet. He stayed where he was so he could think. She sounded like another Valerie. The last thing he wanted was to lose his heart again to someone who would eventually leave for greener pastures.

"I'm just saying. I'll give you her number. You call her. Take her out on a nice date."

"I don't want to get both our hopes up," he said.

"It's one date. Do you have anything better planned?"

No, he didn't. He got up and ran the faucet to check his work. It wouldn't kill him to be social. "Fine. Give her my number and have her call me."

"No." His mother put her hand on her chest and shook her head. "That would be wrong. She's not like one of your cowgirls. She's a nice girl."

"Cowgirls?" he asked, crooking his eyebrow.

"The ones you keep staring at on your phone."

*Busted.*

"I'm a fan of women's rodeo, that's all."

He was a fan of pretty cowgirls. June Grayson. Shayna James. Betty Anders.

Shaking her finger at him, his mother said, "This girl is real. Not some fantasy. Sofia has been very sheltered, and it would be too forward of her to call a strange man."

"But going out on a date with one is okay?" Esteban wiped his hands on a towel. He was getting a bad feeling about this.

"That's different. You'll come to church with me on Sunday and I'll introduce you to her family."

"I'm working on Sunday."

His mother made a disgusted sound. "You work too much, especially for an assistant foreman who doesn't have hiring responsibility. I hear Galveston has a lot of jobs for men with your experience."

"I like Last Stand. I like the Three Sisters Ranch." He frowned down at the list. "Where are Sam and Luis? They could be doing most of this for you."

"Luis is helping your sister out with the baby."

Esteban looked up in alarm. "Everything okay?"

"Cliff has been drinking again." His mother grabbed his arm before he could march over to his sister's place and beat the shit out of his brother-in-law. "They're back in counseling. That's where they are now. Luis is taking Dina to the renaissance fair so Cliff and Beatriz can have some time to work through this."

"Give me twenty minutes alone with Cliff and I'll settle it." Esteban's fists were still clenched with the need to pound some sense into his sister's selfish husband. Their seven-year-old daughter deserved a better father.

"Things like this happen in marriages. You can't interfere."

"Watch me," Esteban said between his teeth. He had held back the first time Cliff relapsed and spent the weekend in Vegas, losing big and probably cheating on Beatriz. The second time, Beatriz made Esteban promise not to hurt him, so he just yelled and threatened Cliff as the slimy bastard had cowered and begged for forgiveness. Three times was definitely not the charm, but this go-round, Esteban wasn't going to give his mother or his sister a heads-up of what he was going to do. This time he was going to haul Cliff out behind the barn and kick the ever-loving shit out of him.

"Sam is with Anne. They're looking at apartments where they can live in sin."

That broke him out of his vengeful thoughts. Esteban jumped in to defend his brother and his high school sweetheart. "They're planning on getting married, eventually. It's just not the right time."

"Why not?"

"Well to begin with, they both just graduated. They've got their whole lives ahead of them."

"Anne has a good job. And Sam will too, once your ranch hires him. I can't see why they have to rush into this apartment thing."

"Let them do what they want." Esteban had left the day he turned eighteen. He wanted to be on his own rather than sharing a room with his two younger brothers. Instead, he sometimes got to share a house with eleven other men when the Three Sisters Ranch was at full capacity.

"Then it's time they got married." His mother stomped back down the stairs.

Esteban let her cool off and he fixed a shelf in his mother's closet while he was there. His mother was obsessed with marrying them all off. She'd taken it as a personal insult when he didn't marry Valerie. If he had left to go live in Dallas, he'd have had to find a corporate job like Valerie had, and that just wasn't him. He would have had to uproot his entire life and move away from his friends and family. Valerie said he didn't love her enough to do that. Maybe he hadn't. She had called him selfish. Maybe he was. She complained he was being stubborn. That part was true, but there was nothing he could do about it.

When he stepped out of the closet, his mother was standing there waiting for him with her arms crossed.

"You need to talk some sense into your brother."

"Which one?" Esteban asked.

"Samuel," she said, putting her hands on her hips. "You tell him that he can get married at the town hall and have a big wedding later. I don't want him to live with Anne unless they're married."

"Sam and Anne are adults. If they want to get married, they will."

Personally, Esteban thought eighteen was too young to

get married. But he wasn't the expert on the subject, so he kept that opinion to himself.

"It's not right." His mother shook her head and her eyes filled up with tears. "I love Anne like she's my own daughter. I know she loves him, and he loves her. It doesn't make any sense. Why can't they be married before moving in together?"

"Mamá, calm down."

Yeah, that was the wrong thing to say.

"Calm down?"

Esteban slumped against the door. He needed to learn to think before he opened his mouth. His mother lapsed into Spanish and treated him to a good ten minutes of why she thought he and his brothers were going straight to hell and it was up to her to stop it, any way she could. She ended by taking a deep breath and saying, "Do you understand me?"

"I'll talk to Sam," he said wearily.

"What about Luis?"

"What did he do?" Esteban must have missed that during the tirade. He hoped it wouldn't set her off again.

"I want him to become a priest."

That was just too much for him. Esteban walked around her and headed down the stairs.

"Did you hear what I said?"

"Does Luis want to be a priest?"

"No, he wants to dance all night, every night, at that Hickory Hall place."

That actually sounded like fun.

"And you know the kind of girls that hang out at places

like that."

"Cowgirls," he said, forcing himself to keep a straight face. He almost lost it when she narrowed her eyes at him.

"Luis needs to be more responsible," she said.

"That I can agree with. But if he doesn't have the calling, he can't be a priest."

She seemed to accept that logic.

"He can start by helping out with this chore list. Tell him I said to weed your garden and water the plants." Esteban looked down at his list. "And why can't he go shopping with you? Not that I mind taking you on my day off, but there could be better things we could be doing."

"I save it up because I want to spend some time with you," his mother said. "Do you think we could go to Valencia's for lunch while we're in town?"

And just like that, the storm was over. That was the story of his life: one moment his mother was a raging firebrand, and the next moment a sweet old lady.

"I think we could arrange that," Esteban said, smiling at her.

After finishing up a few more items on the list that he didn't trust his brothers not to half-ass, he drove his mother into town so she could do some shopping and socializing. He glanced at his watch. Nate should be at the chow wagon by now and if he was eating, he'd hear his phone and answer it if Esteban called him. His mother wouldn't give him a moment's peace if he didn't keep trying to get his brothers jobs.

Leaning up against the outside wall of the grocery store,

Esteban phoned his boss.

"Why are you calling me on your day off?" Nate asked in lieu of the traditional hello.

Esteban was used to Nate Pierson's gruff attitude. He was the foreman at the Three Sisters Ranch and Esteban was his second-in-command. It used to bother him that Nate wasn't a talker, but he got over it fast. Nate valued hard work and results. Chitchat seemed to piss him off, so Esteban got right to the point.

"Sam and Luis are looking for work and we've got a lot of it."

"Unless they're volunteering, we don't have the money to pay them."

Esteban tamped down his frustration. All the remaining ranch hands had been working long, hard hours for months now. Things were getting better, but they were still short-staffed. "When do you think we can get some help?"

"I'll talk to Emily again. Maybe I can squeeze her for one extra person. Which one of your brother's is your favorite?"

He didn't play favorites, but this job would keep Luis out of Hickory Hall most nights and maybe get his mother off the priest kick. "They've both worked ranches before, part-time here and there. If I can only pick one, I can flip a coin."

"Do that."

Esteban knew that tone. There would only be one job opening and even that was probably pushing it. "Luis. He can start immediately."

"I'll let you know. Enjoy your day off." Nate hung up on

him.

It was a start.

Peeking into the store, Esteban saw his mother chatting animatedly with Delilah Corbyn, the owner and chef of Dragonfly, a farm-to-table restaurant in town. This was going to take a while. Sitting down on a nearby bench, Esteban scrolled through social media while he waited.

He wasn't much for the social part of social media. He liked posting pictures he took of the cattle ranch. He wasn't as good as Kelly Sullivan, who had a portrait studio on the Three Sisters Ranch, but he did all right.

Mostly, he liked looking at pictures of pretty girls on social media. Cowgirls, in particular. He followed the Women's Pro Rodeo Circuit on all their accounts and checked them daily. Shayna James had some great pictures, but ever since she hooked up with that *pendajo* Dustin Greaves, her feed was all weddings and flowers and shit. Not his scene at all. The Grayson sisters hadn't been posting much. They were from Last Stand, Texas, and he and every other hand on the Three Sisters Ranch followed their careers closely.

His favorite was June. One of these days, he'd get up enough nerve to introduce himself to her when she came back to town. The trick was fighting through the throng of partygoers to even get close to her. Esteban had had a crush on her since high school, when he'd seen her ride for the first time.

Her hair had been bright pink back then, and she'd had a nose ring. She'd been so "in your face" with her hell-raising attitude that she'd caught his attention and his heart immediately. June hadn't posted in a while, and she had missed a bunch of events. There were rumors on the chat boards that she had gotten busted for something and tossed into jail, but he didn't believe it. Still, he thought as he thumbed through some glamour shots she'd posted, the Three Sisters Ranch was boarding her horse, Athena. He'd seen Emily riding the mare a few times. There had to be a reason why June didn't have her horse with her, wherever she was.

He'd heard another rumor that June would be coming back to Last Stand for Emily's wedding at the end of the month. Merry would probably come too, because the Last Stand Rodeo was the week after. Maybe, he'd get up enough courage to see if June would go out for a beer with him.

As he was staring into June Grayson's deep brown eyes and wishing the smile she was flashing at the camera was directed at him, a woman sat down next to him, almost too close for comfort.

He shifted to frown at her and had to do a double take. He looked at the woman. Looked at the phone. Looked back at the cowgirl sitting next to him.

"June Grayson?" Esteban said, frozen in shock.

"In the flesh."

She was just as gorgeous in person as she was in photos. Her sandy-brown hair was tinged with pink highlights and he caught a tantalizing glimpse of a tattoo on the curve of her leg when she crossed them. She wore a frothy pastel sundress that looked like it was made of cotton candy.

"Hi," he said unintelligently.

She held out her hand for him to shake. He was a little surprised at her firm grip and the calluses on her palm. She looked so much like a fashion model, he had forgotten that she spent most of her life on the back of a horse, just like he did.

"I was wondering if you could help me with a joke," she said.

Esteban nodded, wondering if the joke was on him, and not caring.

"You look like you've got steady hands." She leaned in and he caught a whiff of men's cologne. It was familiar and he realized it was the same type he used.

June Grayson smelled like him. And up close, she had lips he wanted to cover with his own. He shifted, his pants suddenly tight. "Steady."

"There's some danger involved." She licked her lips and that glimpse of her little pink tongue nearly dropped him.

"Dangerous? Danger is my middle name."

Oh no. He did not just say that. Brain first. Mouth second. When would he ever learn?

"Mine's trouble."

"I can see that," he said. "What do you need?"

"I need to reenact a scene from my wild younger days."

"How wild?"

"I rode my horse naked down Main Street."

Esteban choked on air.

"And I need you to film it for my TikTok."

"I think that violates the terms of Tik..." Esteban shut up. *Why am I trying to talk her out of this?* "Yeah, of course,

I'll film you."

"Great." She leaned in and kissed him quick on the mouth and then popped up before he could react. "Here," she said. "Press the button as soon as you see me."

"You got it," he said.

"It'll be like herding the longhorns, only better."

"You got that right." Esteban looked around for the hidden camera and waited for Ringo or Frenchie to jump out and jeer at him for falling for this. But they were out riding the back forty with Nate, and were far away from here.

This was happening. June Grayson—June Freakin' Grayson—had kissed him, and now she was darting down Laurel Street. He stood up, wondering how he could stop traffic so that she and her horse didn't get caught up in it. His lips tingled from her kiss. He wanted more.

"*Mijo*, are you ready?" his mother asked, coming out of the shop.

*Not now.*

"I just need a few minutes. Why don't you go to the car, and I'll meet you there?" He started fast walking toward Laurel Street.

"Esteban, where are you going?"

Seeing the horse's head, Esteban lifted the phone and zoomed in as best as he could. This had to be a trick, a publicity stunt. She'd come into view in a WPRC bikini or something.

"Holy shit," he breathed.

June wore only her Bad Reputation Stetson.

His mother screamed.

Traffic stopped.

His hand never shook, but he couldn't take his eyes off her soft curves, and the creamy expanse of her skin. She had long, toned legs with a tattoo of a bucking horse on her thigh. Her belly was perfection. He wanted to lick his way up to the long, graceful line of her neck.

She tossed a few flyers at gawkers. Esteban tried to zoom in on them. Bachelorette party? Could it be she was doing this for Emily's party?

"Esteban," his mother shrieked. "Don't film that."

"It's okay, Mamá. It's her phone. She asked me to do this."

"What?" she screeched.

He was probably going to pay for this later, but damn, it was so worth it.

June rode astride Athena, clip-clopping down Main Street. She waved happily at everyone and handed out more flyers. Esteban needn't have worried about the cars. They stopped dead in the street.

She rode her horse slowly toward him and came up alongside.

"You... You..." his mother stammered. "You put on some clothes, young lady."

Holding out her hand for her phone, June winked at him. "Did you get it?"

He nodded, trying desperately to maintain eye contact. But he was only human. Up this close he saw she was wearing flesh-colored pasties over her nipples and the thinnest G-string he had ever seen, not that he was a connoisseur of those type of things.

"Come by Callum's Country Party House after the bachelorette party tonight and I'll buy you a drink," she said.

"He most certainly will not," his mother said, pulling on his arm. Good luck with that—he outweighed her by a good seventy-five pounds.

"See you there," Esteban said.

"Esteban Alejandro Cristobal Lopez," his mother said threateningly.

June tipped her hat at him and turned Athena around. The back view was just as nice as the front. He never thought he'd be envious of a saddle.

The whoop of a siren jolted him out of his thoughts as Police Chief Highwater pulled his squad car down Main Street, just as she turned back down Laurel.

His mother grabbed his ear and twisted.

"Ow, Mamá." Esteban struggled free.

"Let's go," she said, seething.

Somehow, he didn't think she'd be setting him up with Sofia after all. And that was just fine with him.

# Chapter Three

"WERE YOU DRUNK?" her sister April asked, after she picked June up from the police station.

"No, just bored." June had had a blast. It was the first time she had felt like her old self in a long time.

"You're just lucky that it was a school day. Do you know you could have had to register with the sex offenders list if you exposed yourself to a child?"

"It was a joke," June groaned. "I made people laugh and clutch their pearls. It was the best day ever."

"You're crazy. You're going viral and for all the wrong reasons."

"What's the worst that could happen? I get fired from the WPRC?" Been there, done that, wore the Stetson today just to cram it up their ass when they saw it on TikTok.

"According to the lawyer I talked to, six months in county and a thousand-dollar fine."

"No one has any sense of humor anymore." June sighed. "I wore a thong, and my nips were covered. But even if I hadn't, being topless is legal in Texas. They can't pin an indecent exposure rap on me because my hoo-ha wasn't showing."

"Barely."

"You worry too much."

"And you don't worry about anything."

"So together, we even each other out." And that was pretty much their relationship in a nutshell. They would never see eye to eye on anything, but they'd always have each other's backs. "It all worked out. Nobody got hurt and in the end, I put a lot of smiles on people's faces." Of course, there were a lot of frowns as well, but June didn't count them.

"Then why were you arrested?"

"Littering and disorderly conduct."

"Oh no. What did you do?"

"I mouthed off to Highwater."

April squinted at her. "You have been drinking."

"No. I wouldn't ride Athena if I was drunk," June said. "She might have gotten hurt. Anyway, I apologized to Highwater. Emily came and got Athena with her horse trailer, but she couldn't give me a ride home because she had stuff to do and I didn't want to drag my sorry ass all over Last Stand. Mama's working, so I called you."

"Does Mama know what you did?"

"Who do you think brought me back my clothes?"

April banged her head on the steering wheel. "You can't do things like this."

"Well, not anymore. I had to promise not to streak across Main Street ever again. In return, Highwater is going to drop the charges."

"June, no one is going to hire you after they hear about this stunt."

June didn't want to think about being tied down to a stodgy place and she certainly didn't want to be indoors any more than she had to be.

"I've got a lead on a job."

"Where?" April asked.

"That's where you come in."

"I'm not getting naked."

"No one asked you to. Look, I just need you to talk to Cole and see if Trent is willing to have me there to teach girls wanting to learn barrel racing from a pro."

"If you hadn't pulled your Lady Godiva shtick today, you might have had a better shot."

"I did it for Emily."

April shook her head. "Oh bullshit. You were looking for a reason to take your clothes off."

"Maybe I was. But it was fun."

"I'll ask Cole. But don't get your hopes up. They don't get many girls at the school."

"Maybe I can change that. Or maybe I'll ask Emily to hire me on as a ranch hand."

"That's some serious hard work. Cole moonlights a few days a month and he's always exhausted. Are you sure you're up for it?"

"I sat on my ass for three months in that rehab facility. It'll be good to get outside and ride all day."

April shook her head. "You always have to do things the hard way, don't you?"

"That's just the way things turn out for me."

"Please don't go crazy tonight," April said. "You know

how you get when you're drinking."

"First of all, I'm not going to be drinking, and second of all, I'm looking forward to this. Don't shit all over it."

"I'm not. I just want what's best for you."

"How can you know that, when I don't even know what that is?"

June was also looking forward to seeing that cute cowboy tonight. She should have gotten his name. The old woman behind him was screaming it. Alejandro? Chris? June shook her head. She couldn't remember. "I looked great, though. Did you see the video?" June had uploaded it everywhere before Chief Highwater caught up with her and wrapped her in one of those blankets that looked like tin foil.

"No," April said, snorting.

"Do you think Dustin is going to see it?"

"Why would you want your ex to see it?"

"So he can be reminded of what he gave up when he asked Shayna James, Princess of Pain, to marry him."

"Are you pissed off about that?"

*Was she?* "No," June decided. "I'm pissed off that he cheated and that I was dumb enough to agree to have an exclusive relationship. But I'm never getting married. So if he and Shayna want to chase that happily-ever-after scam, I wish them all the best that karma has to offer them. I'm glad to be away from them and all the drama."

But she wasn't glad to be away from the rodeo.

They drove back to Mama's trailer and then sat in silence for a few moments.

"I am pissed about how the WPRC handled the situation," June grumbled. "I didn't need to go to rehab."

April shrugged. "I think it helped."

"Maybe a little," June admitted. She'd hated being cooped up in the rehab center, though. She hadn't minded the counseling part. It was the cold, sterile environment that she hadn't been able to stand.

"Are you going to try and get Dustin back?"

"Hell no. He blew his chance."

"Have you asked the WPRC to reinstate you?"

"They're not returning my calls. And I think Sinclair Thompson blocked my number."

April handed June her phone.

After a moment's consideration, June looked up his number and called him from April's phone.

"Sinclair Thompson," he answered on the first ring.

Rage fought with the need to be professional. "I want you to reconsider the decision to have me retire," she said and was pleased that her voice didn't shake with suppressed emotion.

Sinclair sighed heavily. "Ms. Grayson, I'll be blunt. You don't fit our image."

"Oh, but Shayna James using a cattle prod on her horse does?"

"Your hatred of Shayna has made you a volatile competitor."

June set her jaw. "And your favoritism of her is suspect. She had to take anger management classes and she's still allowed to compete. How is that different from my counseling sessions?"

"If Shayna gets on her horse angry, it's not the same risk as if you get on your horse drunk," he said viciously.

April winced.

"I have never ridden my horse under the influence," June said slowly and deliberately. "Shayna, on the other hand, can't win a round without cheating and inflicting pain on her horse."

"I'm not listening to this nonsense."

"It's not nonsense. Ask any other rider."

But he had hung up on her.

"And now you're blocked," June said, handing her sister back her phone.

"He's a real piece of work," April said. "You're better off without him."

"I'm going to get back into the circuit," June vowed. "And if I have to run over Sinclair Thompson to do it, that's even better."

"Well, don't do it tonight. If you get arrested, I can't come bail you out. Cole and I have plans."

"You're leaving the bachelorette party early?"

"It's not my scene anyway. Besides, he's been working at Trent's school during the day and at another ranch overnight for the past two weeks. We haven't had a lot of time together."

"Date night, huh?" June said, getting out of the car and stretching.

"I hope I can stay awake," April grumbled.

"Start drinking coffee now."

"Then I'll be peeing all night."

"TMI." June waved as April backed out of the driveway.

June was pleased that she'd stood up for herself. Her therapist would have been proud, too. Talking to Sinclair had loosened some of the anger that had lodged in her gut like a rock. And flashing her goods down Main Street had made her feel like her old self again. The only problem with acting and feeling like her old self, though, was that she had to make sure she didn't fall back into any bad habits. Bad habits…like going out to a bar for a bachelorette party and having a drink or two. Or like taking a stripper home.

June was a little worried about tonight, especially if the locals offered to buy her a celebratory drink or wanted to go shot for shot with her the way she'd done in the past. She didn't want to explain why she was dry because she didn't want the whole town talking about her problems. On the other hand, she could have a few drinks and not get blackout drunk. There had to be a middle road she could take.

"Ugh." June leaned her head back and screamed at the sky. That wound up scaring the shit out of her mother's pony, Tulip. "Sorry, girl," she said as Tulip stared at her, wild-eyed.

Overthinking things was April's gig, not hers. June wanted to make sure that she still knew how to have fun without alcohol. If it got too difficult being at the bachelorette party with the booze, she could just leave.

But first, she needed to talk to someone. June dialed the number that her counselor from rehab had given her. Almost as soon as the phone rang, it was immediately answered.

"Rats, I was hoping that I would have to leave a message," June said.

"That sounds like you're trying to hide what you're doing from me, but still get the credit for calling me first." Linda had been her counselor in the rehab center, and accepted absolutely no bullshit from anyone. That was too bad, because June was very good at bullshit.

"I road my horse down Main Street today," June announced. "I was naked." She was almost naked, but it made for a more dramatic line to take out the qualifiers.

"Again?" Linda quipped. "How about we discuss doing things that will help you break out of this destructive cycle that you've found yourself in over the last couple of years?"

"That's what this was. I was feeling a little disconnected from myself. So I did something wild and crazy to bring me back."

"How did that work out for you?"

"I wound up getting arrested, but I got out of it."

"Oh, June…" Linda said.

June could just picture her shaking her head, resting her fingers on her temples.

"It's all good, but that's not the reason why I'm calling. I met a guy, today… Well, I didn't really meet him. Emily had stuff to do before her bachelorette party tonight, so I needed someone to film my great ride for social media. I invited him to come to Callum's Country Party House tonight, after the bachelorette party."

"Tell me about this place," Linda said.

"It's like a Western-themed indoor amusement park. In one section, there are games like pool, and air hockey, and a wall of arcade classics like Buck Hunter. Then there's the karaoke bar."

"A bar?"

"With dancing," June said helpfully.

"Did you really call to ask me if I thought this was a bad idea?"

"No, I'm pretty sure it is a bad idea. I'm going to go anyway. I called to ask your permission."

"June, even if I wanted to give you permission, I wouldn't. This is your recovery. This is your journey. You are an adult capable of making decisions like this on your own. However, if you'd like my opinion…?"

Why did she have to put it all back on her? June scowled as she let herself into the trailer. "Yeah, I'd like some advice, too."

"My opinion is you should stick with your pregnant friend tonight at the bachelorette party. What was her name again?"

"Kelly," June said. But the problem with that was Kelly would probably go home early and June knew that if she left the party, she would have some crippling FOMO. Not to mention, she'd miss out on seeing her sexy cowboy. If he even showed up. She said as much to Linda.

"Go home early," Linda said. "Then call him up tomorrow and meet him for coffee."

"Coffee shops are boring, and they don't have dancing." And she hadn't got his number.

"Are you going to be tempted to have a drink at this place?" Linda asked.

"Yes, but I have it all planned out. I'm going to order a large seltzer and sip on it all night long."

"That sounds like a very healthy choice. What are you going to do when you're tempted to get just one beer, or do just one shot?"

"I've never used to drink as hard as I did that one time," June said. "I did it then because I was really mad, and I wanted to forget how bad things were for a little while. That's never going to happen again. I'd rather feel the pain in the moment and get it over with. I never want to wake up the next morning and wonder what happened to me. So, I don't think you have to worry about me, like you have to worry about the others."

"I'm not worried about any of my patients," Linda said. "You're all capable individuals who can make their own decisions and deal with the consequences of their actions. Do you have plans on what to do if you happen to relapse and become too drunk to drive?"

"That's not going to happen. But if it does, I'll call my sister, or my mother, or an Uber. There's no way I'm going to get behind the wheel if I have a couple of shots and beer. But I'm not going to." June sat down at her bed and glared at the wall. How many times did she have to repeat herself?

"Do you have a plan for getting through tonight sober?"

They had discussed in therapy ways to visualize success. At first, June had thought it was hokey, but it actually worked.

"I'm going to slip in late, so my entrance doesn't take away from Emily's party. I'm going to stay in the background, nursing my seltzer. If I get recognized and someone offers to buy me a drink, I'll ask for a Shirley Temple."

"What if someone tries to force a drink on you?"

"Force me? I'd slap it out of his hand, because it's probably doctored with a date rape drug or something."

"That's not quite what I meant. I meant if you run into a fan who wants to toast your victory or an old friend who wants to have a drink with you, for old times' sake. How are you going to handle it?"

"Well, I can't be rude."

"It's not rude to say, no thank you," Linda said.

"Yeah, but sometimes they take it that way and it's easier just to accept the drink," June said. And it was hard to turn down free drinks, which was probably how she'd ended up in rehab to begin with.

"Here's a little trick to try. Tell them that you're not feeling well and want to stick with soda. Most people don't want anyone who isn't feeling well to get sicker, so that could get you off the hook."

June snapped her fingers. "I got a better idea. Why don't I tell them that I'm allergic to alcohol?"

"Stay away from the big lies. It gets difficult to keep track of them, and also, it's been well documented that you are not allergic."

"Okay, good point." June thought it made a better story, but she supposed it was easier not to dig a hole for herself, if she could avoid it.

"What do you want to do at the bachelorette party that doesn't involve drinking?"

"See a bunch of people I haven't talked with in a while. Dance. Celebrate Emily. Maybe hit on a stripper or two. Then hopefully afterwards, I'll get lucky with the hunky cowboy who I roped into acting as my cameraman this afternoon."

"Not literally, I hope."

"I didn't have a place to put my rope. Remember, I was naked."

Linda sighed. "It sounds like you're going to be too busy tonight to think about drinking. Just stay hydrated. Keep a glass of water in your hand when you're not on the dance floor. How late are you planning on staying out?"

"Are you my mom now?"

"No, I'm asking because the later it gets and the more tired you feel, the more it can affect your judgment."

"I'll call it an early night at midnight. Does that work for you?"

"Does that work for *you*?" Linda countered.

June made a face. She hated owning up to the responsibility. That meant that any mistakes were hers and hers alone. Of course, it also meant that she could claim the victories, too. "Yeah, I think that's a good plan."

"What if your hot cowboy wants to stay up later?"

"I hope that's the case. I'll bring him back to… Shoot, I forgot; I don't have a hotel room. I can't bring him back home with me to my mom's trailer." That was another reason she needed a job as soon as possible. She smoothed a hand over her childhood comforter. It had cowboys riding bucking broncos on it. "I guess we'll have to go back to his place."

"Be careful. If you do go back to his place, make sure someone knows where you are. And if you have been drinking, you may want to call April or your mom to let them know what's happening, just in case things go too far."

"If I go back to his house, I want things to go too far."

"And if he offers you a drink?"

"I'll tell him, I'm not there to talk and we should get right to it. I'll spare you the details."

"I appreciate that," Linda said. "I also appreciate that you called me today."

"Well, a promise is a promise," June said. When she'd left rehab, Linda had asked her to call her anytime, day or night, if she needed some help. "You and I both know I'm not an alcoholic, but I could probably have seen myself heading that way if it hadn't been for you and the center."

"Don't concern yourself with labels. You're doing the best you can."

*Am I?*

"I talked to Sinclair Thompson today. Asked him if I could come back to the WPRC. He said no fucking way."

"How did that make you feel?"

"Sad. Angry. Confused. Mean."

"Mean?"

"I want to earn getting thrown out, you know?" June kicked the bed in frustration.

"Maybe you should write a letter pleading your case. Go over his head."

Nodding, June rubbed her toe. "Thanks for listening."

Her sisters were great, and even Mama was understanding, but they tended to talk more than listen. And they had a habit of making decisions for her because she was the baby of the family. June found herself wanting to do the exact opposite of whatever they said, just to prove she was in charge. She wanted to talk more about her anger with Sinclair, but they'd be on the phone forever and June had a party to get ready for. There was always next week. "I'll give you call tomorrow and let you know how it went."

"No matter how it went, I will not judge you. I'm here to help. I respect all of your choices and decisions."

"I'm glad someone does," June said, getting off the phone.

After ransacking her closet, she came up with a cute little number that was all fringe and sparkles. It had a flared skirt, so that when she twisted and twirled, it would fan out. Cushioned socks and her best cowboy boots went on next. She thought about asking her mother to do her hair, but after a few hours of dancing, it would all be hanging down her face anyway.

Checking her social media accounts, June was pleased she had received a lot of likes and a couple of people requesting to have the sensor bars taken off of certain areas in her post. It made her feel good, and she hoped Shayna James was gnashing her teeth over it, and Dustin was regretting what he'd lost.

"No, I don't wish that all," June said to her full-length mirror. Dustin and Shayna had no business renting space in her head. They were her past, and this was her future. It didn't have to be dull. She could make it whatever she wanted it to be. It didn't have to include alcohol. It didn't have to include sex. But it had to be something more than just sitting in her mama's trailer watching TV and hoping that the WPRC changed their mind. While she was ready to move on from Dustin and Shayna, she wasn't quite ready to move on from the rodeo and Sinclair Thompson.

# Chapter Four

J UNE RECITED WHAT she was going to do in her head. Walk in. Get a seltzer. Get lots of blackmail pictures of Emily. Have fun. Flirt outrageously. Find a cowboy. Dance until she dropped.

"That's a good plan," she said to herself.

Not wanting to steal Emily's thunder, June was fashionably late to the bachelorette party. Leaving the Bad Reputation Stetson at home, she wore her hair down. If it got too annoying later on in the evening, she'd just pull it back into a ponytail.

She walked past the gaming section without being recognized, but as soon as she ordered her seltzer, two men on either side of her clapped her on the back and congratulated her.

"You and your sister are the best rodeo cowgirls I've ever seen," the man on her left said.

"I remember that one time when you almost got thrown by a horse…"

"That wasn't me," June said, arching her neck to see where the bachelorette party was. It looked like they were in the back. Callum's had partitioned a large section off from the crowd with a floor-to-ceiling accordion-type divider, but she could see people she knew opening up the partition and slipping through. "Athena has never tried to throw me in her entire life." Her brother Ares had done a number on April, but not in competition.

"That wasn't you?" the man on her right said. "Got her foot caught in the stirrups, but pulled herself up and continued on with the race?"

"Nope. Must be another barrel racer. We all look alike." She started to move away, but he shifted his body to stop her.

"Let me buy you a drink."

*Here we go*, June thought. "That's really kind of you, but I've got one." She tried to step around him, but this time, the other guy blocked her. She tamped down annoyance.

"Seltzer? I had you figured for a whiskey woman."

"Not lately," she said. "Seltzer really quenches my thirst. Now, if you'll excuse me, my friends are waiting for me." June readied herself for a bar fight, wishing she had a bottle to smash dramatically on the bar.

"Mike, Andy, fuck off."

She looked up and saw her handsome cowboy from this afternoon standing just behind them.

"Or what?" the one on the left asked belligerently.

The other one nudged him hard with his elbow. "Hey, Esteban. Are you hiring?"

So, his name was Esteban. June took advantage of his distraction to eye him up and down. He had warm brown eyes and wavy hair to match. Long and lanky, he stood tense on the balls of his feet, ready for a fight if it came down to it. June admired the slow play of muscles underneath his black cotton shirt. His blue jeans were tight in all the right places and she couldn't wait to get him alone.

"Maybe." Esteban looked at June. "Are these dickheads bothering you?"

"No," she said. "They're fans. But I've got a bachelorette party to get to and…" She let her sentence trail off.

Mike and Andy moved aside, which was rather anticlimactic.

"Look us up when you're done," one of them said.

"Yeah, we'll be here all night."

"Great." June gave them a quick smile. Not a chance in hell.

"You're late," Esteban said as they walked away together. "I've been waiting for you."

His slow grin was surprisingly sexy, and she felt the fluttering of something she knew could lead to trouble if she acted on it.

Then again, hadn't she just been lamenting how dull her life was becoming? Esteban was tall and had the type of muscles you got from tossing hay bales and wrangling cattle all day. And he had a rugged jaw that had the barest hint of stubble on them.

"You're early," she said. "The bachelorette party's not going to be over until two or so."

"Maybe I couldn't wait to see you."

She turned and stepped in close to him. "Is that true?"

His answer shouldn't matter to her. After all, if she was

looking for a good time, there were plenty of other men out there if he turned her down. And yet, there was a spark between them that she hadn't even remotely felt with anyone since Dustin. Maybe it was the way Esteban looked at her, as if she was the most fascinating woman he'd ever seen. Maybe she was starved for attention.

"Mostly." He laid a hand on her back as they made their way through the restaurant section. "My boss needed me to drive his wife Janice here."

"Nate Pierson's your boss? You work at the Three Sisters Ranch?"

"Yes, ma'am."

"Call me June."

His long silky eyelashes closed for a moment longer than a blink and when he opened up his eyes, she caught her breath at the hot look in his gaze. "June."

This time, his grin coiled into something on the edge of a smolder and her toes tingled. Wow, he was potent up close. If she had met him on the circuit, she would have let him buy her a few drinks and see where it took them.

Drinks, right. She couldn't do that anymore. Frowning, she looked away. Could she even relax enough to let her guard down without that familiar numbing buzz?

"Everything okay?" he asked.

Clearing her throat, she said, "I could spare a dance or two before I join the party. If you're interested."

"I'm interested."

June tanked her seltzer and placed the empty glass on a table. Esteban led her close to the bachelorette party so they could hear the music enough to dance to it. The DJ was playing some rocking old-school country tunes. For once though, she didn't want to dance fast. She wanted to press her body against Esteban to the beat of a song with a sexy bass line.

It had been three long months since she had sex and being near Esteban made her feel like a horny teenager. It was like she was a black-and-white character and now somebody had brought the crayons.

Esteban whirled and twirled her around and then caught her close against him. She enjoyed being in his arms, but the music wasn't going to switch over to something sweet and romantic. Not at a bachelorette party. After a few songs, Esteban was showing signs of slowing down, although June could have danced all night.

She decided to take pity on him. Going up on her tiptoes, she leaned into his ear and said, "I've got time for a couple of drinks."

"You got it." Esteban went over to the bar, while she grabbed a table. She probably should have offered to get them because she owed him a beer for filming her epic ride down Main Street, but she didn't want to risk being accosted again. It wasn't until he got back with two beers that June realized she should've been more specific about what she wanted to drink.

Esteban must have noticed the look on her face. "I'm sorry. Do you not like beer? I can get you something else."

June wanted to be polite, and she didn't want to offend him. He seemed like a good guy and a great dancer. And she was celebrating, wasn't she? She had a new job opportunity to chase down with Trent. She hadn't gotten charged with indecent exposure. And she was finally feeling like herself again. One beer shouldn't be a problem. She put her hand on the mug and had it halfway to her mouth when a little voice inside her head said, "If you're not an alcoholic, like you keep telling everyone, then prove it by not having this drink." June didn't know whose voice it was. It certainly wasn't Linda's kind of advisement. It sounded like June's own voice, when she was being a bitch.

June put the glass down with a small thud. She might as well get this out in the open now. "Actually, I'm trying not to drink alcohol. I've had some issues with it in the past."

"Oh my gosh, I'm so sorry. I didn't know." Esteban pulled the drink back to him. "I can throw these out and get Cokes if you want?"

"No, it won't bother me if you drink. Seriously. Don't waste the money. I'm just going to go up to the bar and get myself a seltzer."

"I can do that if you want." Esteban looked so miserable that June realized he needed to make this right, even though he had done nothing wrong.

"Get two then. That way we can both have two drinks in front of us and spend more time talking and getting to know each other."

Esteban smiled in relief and went back to the bar.

Meanwhile, June looked at the two beers. She wasn't tempted at all. She liked beer. But it wasn't her favorite drink. Would she have been able to resist if he'd had a bottle of Jack and two glasses? It might have been tougher. She liked the burn of the whiskey. It tasted like freedom. It tasted like victory. But that could be because every time she won, she did a shot. Right now, she was thirsty. And while the beer would quench the thirst, she knew the seltzer water was a better choice.

While waiting for Esteban to come back, she had a couple more arguments with herself on whether having one drink would lead to two drinks, which would lead to a blackout. Or if she could just act normally with her usual pre-blackout alcohol consumption. But she found that she didn't want to take a chance, and she didn't want to disappoint Linda.

But most of all, June didn't want those three months of her life that she spent in the rehab center to be utterly wasted. She should have never been sent there, but she was going to make good use of the information that had managed to sink into her thick head. What was it that Linda had said back in the rehab center? Turn things around so that she could see the positive. Sinclair did her a favor by making her slow down and reassess her life. June considered it. Nope. It was still bullshit and he was an asshole.

Esteban put the two seltzers in front of her and sat back down. "Sorry that took so long. It's getting busy."

"I knew we should have rented the whole place out, but Janice and Kelly didn't think we needed to." She lifted up one of her glasses to his and said, "To us."

"To you, June," he said. They clinked glasses. "Are you sure I'm not keeping you from the party?"

June looked at her watch. "Nah, the strippers don't go on until eleven."

"Are you going to get up and dance, too?"

"Shit yeah," she said, playing with the swizzle stick in her drink. "Can I convince you to take a set?"

He almost snorted his beer. "My sister is in there, as well as my boss's wife. So I don't think that's going to happen."

"You could wear a mask. You could be the masked stripper."

"I'll give you a private show, darlin', but not a public one."

"I'll take you up on that. Don't think I won't." She held his gaze as tingles raced all over her body. If it had been anyone else's party but Emily's, she'd already be taking this cowboy home.

"Keep looking at me like that and you're going to miss the strippers," he said in a low voice that did major things to her hormones.

"It's not a good idea to challenge me." She stared at him with all the lust she felt.

The noise of the bar dropped away and all she could hear was the heavy thump of her heart when she read the same desire staring back at her.

June wasn't sure how long they would have held their steamy gazes before she jumped in his lap, because they were interrupted by three squealing women who wanted to have selfies taken with her. Snapping out of the trance she had been in, June good-naturedly obliged even though she really wanted to spend some time with Esteban alone. But she owed her fans for all the support they gave her. And hopefully, they would transfer that support to Merry, who needed it now more than ever if she wanted to beat Shayna James in the finals.

"I'm so sorry," she said when the fans left. "That happens every now and then. I suppose the more time I spend hanging around here, the less frequent it'll be."

"It's okay." He reached across the table and rubbed his thumb over her wrist in slow circles. She shivered in reaction. "You're a local hero."

"I'm no Trent Campbell," June said, speaking of Kelly Sullivan's husband. Trent was a big-deal bull rider until he had a career-ending accident with a psycho bull. Unfortunately, Trent didn't get the memo and rode the bull again once he'd healed up.

"Have you had a chance to check out his school?"

June shook her head. She hadn't wanted to do much of anything when she got back to Last Stand. If Athena hadn't been boarded at the Three Sisters Ranch, she probably would have driven out to wherever Merry was and hung around with her, feeling sorry for herself. At least in her mama's home, no one but her mama could see her sulking.

"Your sister's man works there. Cole's a good friend of mine. He teaches the kids who are just starting out. He'll make a good father."

"Please…" June held out her hand. "Let me get through Emily's bachelorette party before we start throwing April a baby shower."

"I don't think that's up to you and me."

"April's too smart to fall into that trap."

Esteban cocked his head. "Trap?"

"Marriage, kids. It's a sucker's bet."

"I don't get what you mean."

"I'm never getting married."

"Never is a long time."

"Marriage is meaningless. It's a piece of paper and a big, expensive party that people feel obligated to attend."

"Have you shared this with Emily?"

"Emily, that traitor, felt the same way...until she met Donovan Link."

"Maybe someone will get you to change your mind, too."

"Even if they did, it would only end up in divorce and bad feelings."

"Wow." Esteban shook his head. "And Emily still has you in the bridal party."

"How do you know about that?" she asked.

"The ranch hands gossip worse than the Last Stand Ladies' Bridge Club."

"What else do they say about me?" June was enchanted by the way he blushed and looked away.

"Like I said, you're a small-town hero. It doesn't hurt that you're gorgeous."

"A fallen hero, but they don't know that yet. I'd appreciate it if you kept what I told you on the down-low. It's complicated and wrapped up with a lot of bad feelings between me and the WPRC."

To her disappointment, he let go of her wrist to pantomime turning a key over his lips. "Your secret is safe with me."

"Now you have to tell me a secret," she said, grabbing his hand back.

"I'm not that exciting," he said.

"I beg to differ. Tell me something about ranch life."

"That's definitely boring."

"All right, what's the craziest thing you've ever done?"

"I think you and I have different definitions of crazy. I've never been naked in public."

"That's a crime," she purred.

"How did everything go with the uploaded video?" Esteban pulled out his phone.

"You're changing the subject," she said in a singsong voice.

"And you're trending on Twitter."

"I am?" June fumbled with her phone. "Hot damn." She looked up at him. "Don't think I've let you off the hook for the questions."

Clearing his throat, Esteban said, "I think you got a couple more followers on Instagram. I made a TikTok account, so I can watch your video whenever I want."

"You liked what you saw?"

"Oh yeah."

"Good," she said smugly. She hadn't started out with a plan of seducing a man today, but it would be the cherry on top of her day.

"Did Highwater give you a hard time?" Esteban asked.

"No more than I deserve. But he dropped the charges as

long as I promised not to do it again. So I need to come up with something wild and crazy that doesn't require me riding a horse down Main Street naked."

"Why?" Esteban asked.

"Why what?" June cocked her head at him.

"Why do you need to come up with something wild and crazy to do?"

That was a good question. She and Linda had talked about it in therapy. "That's just me," she said. "I've always been like that. Emily and I used to go on capers. I'm so happy that TikTok wasn't around then. We managed to escape without getting caught because there was never any video proof. Didn't you ever do stupid stunts when you were a kid?"

He shook his head. "No, didn't have much time for that. I was helping my mom and sister take care of my younger brothers. My father split a little after my twelfth birthday. We haven't seen him in years."

June had to rack her brain. "I think mine is on his second wife in Tallahassee, but I'm not sure." She clinked glasses with him. "To worthless fathers."

"Do your sisters keep in touch with him?"

"No." She frowned. "Why would they?" Then she thought about it. "Oh, he's not their father. We each have different sperm donors."

"That must make Father's Day interesting."

"It's just another day."

"Is that why you're so anti-marriage?"

"I don't see why people need to ruin a good thing with a

piece of paper and legal issues." June shuddered.

"Companionship, great sex, sharing your life with someone…" Esteban tallied the count on his fingers.

She grabbed his hand. "All of which can be had without the ball and chain."

"You don't have to be scared of commitment," he said.

"Why not? It's burned me every time."

"Maybe you just haven't met the right man," Esteban challenged.

June considered him. "Are you proposing?"

He almost spat his drink out but swallowed hard instead. "Would you say yes?" he managed to say once he got his coughing under control.

"It would be wild and crazy," she teased him. "And since I can't flash anyone in the center of town anymore…"

"Did Highwater say anything about being naked on Laurel Street?" Esteban waggled his eyebrows at her.

June threw back her head and laughed. "I like how you think, but the 'naked anywhere in Last Stand' was implied. I don't want to push my luck."

"How long are you in town for?"

That was the question of the month. June shrugged. "I haven't decided yet."

"Well, it was a surprise to see you, with or without your clothes on, in Last Stand. You've been a bit of a recluse."

If she was honest, would she scare him off? Better to find out now. "I was forced to go into rehab to avoid jail time." June blew out a laugh. "That sounds pretty hard core, doesn't it? I was drinking too much and got into a fight. The

WPRC is pissed at me, but I'm working on smoothing things over."

"I'm sorry. That must have been rough. It must feel great to be back home."

"You'd think that," June said. "I sure did. Don't get me wrong. I love Last Stand. It will always be my home. When I'm on the road, I can't wait to come back. But once I'm here, I can't wait to get back on the road. I don't understand it. It's probably just my contrary personality."

"I wouldn't say contrary. More like free-spirited."

"I like that. Free spirit sounds a lot nicer than hellion."

"You could always try wearing a pink Stetson with the word *Angel* stitched on the brim."

June laughed. "Do you want me to get struck down by lightning? Not one of the Grayson women is an angel."

"Only in looks," Esteban said gallantly and clinked his glass to hers again.

"Do you like working at the Three Sisters Ranch?" she asked.

"I do. I started out as a ranch hand and worked my way up. I'm trying to get my brothers to work with me. They just turned eighteen and all they want to be is cowboys."

"I can relate. It is better than working a desk job. I'm not cut out to sit all day and type on the computer...unlike my sister, April. She's an accountant."

"She's good friends with Kelly, right?"

"We three sisters and the Sullivan girls are the same ages. We went to school with each other, before we went our separate ways."

"And now you're all back again in Last Stand and the Three Sisters Ranch."

"Almost," June said, thinking of Merry. "Small world. Small town. Small ranch."

"You don't have to ride it," Esteban groaned.

"Maybe you can take me on a tour sometime."

He nodded. "Name the time and place."

"How about tonight after the party?"

"It's not safe to ride around after dark."

"That's too bad," June said, leaning in for a kiss. "Do you think there's anything else we could do?"

Just before their lips touched, the partition folded back and her mother, Penny, poked her head out. "June, get in here. Emily's been looking for you."

"I'll be right there, Mama," June said, through her teeth.

Penny closed the partition. June sighed. "I wish I didn't have other plans right now."

"I'm free later. Why don't you stop by the ranch? Call me and I can guide you to the bunkhouse."

"I know where it is. But I'd like your number anyway."

After they exchanged phone numbers, Esteban cupped the back of her head and gave her a long, lingering kiss that curled her toes in her boots. Swaying, she held on to his shoulders for support. She didn't want it to end.

"June! Oh shit. Never mind. Just hurry it up," her mother said again.

Esteban laughed and touched his forehead to hers, breaking the kiss.

"So help me," June said. "There's such a thing as too

much family time."

"I feel like I should introduce myself to your mama, now."

"Wait for another time when she's not been drinking. Otherwise, she'll probably grab your ass."

"Thanks for the warning." Esteban kissed her again briefly before moving reluctantly away. "If you're too tired after the party tonight, I'll understand."

"I'll be there," she said.

"Good." Then he turned and walked away.

June watched his grabbable ass saunter out of the bar.

"That's a fine hunk of USDA grade-A beef," her mother said after she walked through the partition.

"You ain't lyin'," June said.

# Chapter Five

A S HE WALKED back out to his truck, Esteban couldn't stop thinking about kissing June, not to mention fantasizing about the way he hoped the rest of the night and early morning would go. He had tomorrow off, and if things went as planned, he and June could sleep late and have breakfast together. But first, he ought to go home and take a nap, so he was ready to pull an all-nighter.

Esteban promised himself that he was just going to drive by his sister's house on the way home. Beatriz was at the bachelorette party. Dina was with their mother, and Cliff should have been at work. But when his mother had told him that Beatriz had asked her to watch Dina overnight, all the bullshit alarms went off in Esteban's head.

*All I'm going to do is drive by the house. If his car is not there, then everything is good.*

But of course, not only was Cliff's car in the driveway, there was also another car, one Esteban didn't recognize, next to it. After parking on the street, he sat in his truck and stared into the windows. The lights were bright on the first floor, and he could see some movement going around inside. Feeling like a stalker, Esteban got out of the truck and closed the door.

He tried to give his brother-in-law the benefit of the doubt. Maybe the contract job he was supposed to be on got canceled. Maybe he was sick. But as each step took him closer and closer to the front door, Esteban knew, without a shadow of a doubt, that Cliff was fucking around.

He tried the door, but it was locked. His sister never locked the door when they were home. She probably should have—it wasn't a safe thing to do—but it was hard to break the habit.

Esteban lifted up the fake plant in the flowerpot on the deck. The spare key was underneath it. It wasn't breaking and entering, he reasoned, if you had a key. Quietly, he turned the key in the lock and then walked in. The sultry sound of a saxophone made Esteban's lip curl in a sneer. Forcing himself to see the proof with his own eyes, Esteban walked into the living room where a pretty girl wearing matching lace underwear danced while Cliff sat in his recliner with a beer and watched.

She screamed when she saw him and tried to cover herself with her hands.

Cliff bolted out of his chair. "This isn't what it looks like."

"Well," Esteban drawled. "That's not your wife."

"Wife?" the woman yelled. "You said you were divorced."

"He lied," Esteban said. Out of the corner his eye, he saw the girl gather up her clothes and run out of the room.

"Jasmine, come on. Don't listen to him. Listen to me."

"No, Jasmine, listen to me. Get out while you can. This man is a drunk, a liar, and a cheat."

"You need to mind your own business," Cliff said, coming up to square off on him.

Esteban grinned wildly. He wanted to take the first shot so badly, but he forced his fist down to his side. It would be worth it to take the hit, just to be on the side of moral righteousness. He'd be able to look his mother and sister in the eye and say, "Cliff hit me first." It didn't mean he wasn't going to goad the shit out of Cliff into throwing the first punch, though. There was moral righteousness, and then there was the need to kick this guy's ass once and for all.

"You're going to break my sister's heart. You're going to break your daughter's heart."

"Leave my family out of this. You have no idea what it's been like being trapped in this house for the last year."

Esteban felt a twinge of sympathy. At least Esteban still had a job and it allowed him to be outside all day. Cliff had lost his warehouse job at the start of the pandemic. Beatriz had always been a stay-at-home mom. He knew they were barely getting by, which made the betrayal of him maxing their credit cards out so much worse, especially when he used the money for something selfish instead of to clothe and feed his family. When Esteban thought of it that way, all sympathy fled.

"That doesn't give you an excuse to cheat on your wife and take food from your baby's mouth."

"It's my money."

"And it's your wife and daughter," he countered.

"You sister and I are getting a divorce. The marriage is over."

"Oh, save it," Esteban said. "You're supposed to be going to counseling."

"That's all your mother's idea. Beatriz and I know it's doomed."

Esteban couldn't believe what he was hearing. "You have a daughter. You owe it to her to..."

Cliff barked out laugh. "To what? Be miserable so she can see what living with two people who can't stand each other feels like?"

Jasmine, fully dressed, hurried by them. "I never want to see you again," she snarled and slammed out of the house.

"See what you did?" Cliff shouted. "Jasmine, honey, wait." Cliff went to follow her, but Esteban stood in his way.

*Do it. Push me. Something.*

"I can't take this anymore," Cliff raged. "Your sister is boring. All she does is cook, clean, and complain. Your mother is a shrew who meddles in everything. And you and your brothers are lazy..."

Esteban hit him hard in the stomach before Cliff could finish that sentence. Doubled over, Cliff staggered to the side. Esteban gave him a hard jab to the jaw and Cliff went down. That had been over too quickly.

"I'm done," Cliff wheezed. "I'm divorcing her and getting full custody of my daughter."

"No court in their right mind will give her to you." Still, Esteban felt an ice-cold drip of fear run down his spine.

"Oh yes, they will. Especially when I tell them how controlling Beatriz is. She won't let Dina take horseback-riding lessons or play team sports."

"That's because you blew the money for that on hookers and gambling," Esteban said between his teeth.

Cliff crawled over to the couch and used it to stand. Leaning against it, he fumbled in his pocket for his phone.

"Don't bother Beatriz." Esteban snorted. "Let her at least have some fun tonight, you selfish piece of shit."

"Hello, police? I've been assaulted in my own home. He's still here. I don't feel safe. Please send a squad car."

"You pussy," Esteban spat out.

"You're going to sit in jail for this." Cliff wagged his phone at him.

"Well," Esteban said. "I might as well earn it." He threw a haymaker at Cliff, who barely dodged out of the way.

"You're crazy," Cliff said, punching him in the face.

Staggering back, Esteban had to cover up as Cliff rained blow after blow on him. For the most part, Esteban managed to block the hits, but Cliff got in a few body shots. Esteban had been on the boxing team at school, so he waited for his chance. A fierce upper cut clacked Cliff's teeth together and left him dazed.

Putting some distance between them, Esteban said, "I'm all for the divorce. She's better off without you, but don't punish your daughter. You're a shitty father, but at least do that much for her. Don't take her away from her family."

"I am her family," Cliff shouted and tackled him to the ground.

They wrestled on the wiry brown carpet, Esteban trying

to throw him off while Cliff did his best to slam Esteban's head into the floor.

"You're a drunk," Esteban snarled, pissed that he couldn't shake him off.

"And you're a mama's boy."

Esteban worked his knee up between them. "But you're a dick." He let Cliff pound him in the face so he could switch positions and use his legs to kick Cliff off him. Rolling to his feet, Esteban noticed his left eye was swelling and he tasted blood.

Cliff didn't seem to be in much of a hurry to come back after him, which was good.

"You need to pack your shit and get out of this house," Esteban said.

"It's my name on the lease. Your sister's the one who's leaving. She can move in with her mother for all I care, but Dina stays with me. Any court will see that having Dina in familiar surroundings will be much better for her."

"You evil bastard." Esteban lunged for him, and they traded blows.

Cliff spit blood out on the carpet. "I can't wait to get rid of the lot of you."

Esteban heard sirens in the distance.

"They're playing your song," Cliff taunted.

"You've got no job. No savings. You're going to be evict-ed soon. How is that a stable environment for Dina?" Esteban said.

"I'll go to where the jobs are."

Cliff was going to take his niece away.

"And when Beatriz is sobbing and begging me not to do this, I'm going to tell her it's all your fault."

Esteban's vision clouded to a red haze of rage, and he wiped the smug smile off his brother-in-law's face.

"THANKS FOR BAILING me out," Esteban said to Trent.

"You're lucky I was around."

"I am. No one else was answering their phone."

They were sitting on Trent's front porch. Esteban was well on his way to being drunk. The ice from the cooler felt good on his swollen knuckles when he reached for another beer.

"At least Cliff is still cooling his heels. Last I heard, Beatriz had turned off her phone. Since Cliff doesn't have a dime to his name, he's likely going to have to spend the night in lockup."

"Unless he can get a bail bondsman to put him on a payment plan," Trent added.

"He's a scumbag," Esteban said. "Can you believe what he said about taking Dina away?"

Esteban had told Trent everything.

"You're lucky he picked up a chair and was hitting you with it when the cops came in."

Wincing, Esteban took a big pull of his beer. "Yeah, I feel real lucky."

"You had no business even being there. What if he pulled a gun on you?"

"He hocked his guns," Esteban said.

"Do you think he's going to go through with the divorce?"

"If he doesn't, Beatriz will."

"She's going to be pissed at you."

"Let her." Esteban shrugged, then cursed when it hurt. "She's better off. Dina too." He made a face. "I hate that they're going to be hurt because of me, though."

"You didn't cause this. Well, this…" Trent gestured at him. "You did. But their marriage problems have nothing to do with you."

"I don't know where it went wrong. They seemed so happy together until they weren't."

"They wanted different things."

That had been his father's excuse. Esteban could see a lot of his father in Cliff. He wondered if that was why Beatriz had been initially drawn to him. "This is going to kill my mother. She doesn't believe in divorce. She's still married to my father."

"Where's he these days?"

"Who cares?" Esteban hadn't seen him since before Dina was born. He wasn't even sure he knew he had a grandchild. "Beatriz wanted Dina to have a home with both parents."

"You didn't make Cliff cheat."

"No, but me catching him in the act was the last straw for him. How am I going to make this better?"

"You can't," Trent said. "But you can be there for your family."

Esteban snorted. "Yeah, if I'm not in jail."

"A good lawyer will get you a fine and community service."

"And a bad one will get me two years."

"It's in Cliff's best interest to drop the charges against you, if you drop the charges against him."

"Those charges are the only thing that's keeping him from taking Dina away," Esteban said. If he had to go to jail to keep his niece safe, he would.

"Don't sacrifice yourself. Get a moderator, a family counselor, and talk it out."

Esteban peeled the label off his beer, trying to get it to come off in one piece. "Yeah, Cliff should be more reasonable when he's not drunk and cockblocked. Do you think Nate's going to be pissed at me?"

"Well, you didn't do it while you were on the clock. And you weren't wearing your Three Sisters Ranch T-shirt, so I think he'll be okay with it. If you decide to be stubborn and go to jail for a few years, though, all bets are off."

"I just hope I didn't fuck up Luis's chances of getting hired. We need the help, and Luis needs a job."

"Even if Nate was pissed off at you, he wouldn't take it out on your brother. Besides, Cliff Baker has been asking for the ass whooping you gave him for years now."

They drank in silence for a few minutes, Trent slowly rocking in the porch swing and Esteban slouched in a papasan chair he was pretty sure he wasn't ever getting out of. He checked his phone to see what time it was. It was just after one in the morning.

"Got a hot date?" Trent asked.

"Actually, I do. June Grayson."

"You risked missing a date with a Grayson sister to fight your brother-in-law?"

"I didn't think the prick would call the cops."

"If he'd thought he'd get his ass hauled in too, he wouldn't have," Trent said.

"Do you know June from your circuit days?" Esteban asked, trying to stifle a hint of jealousy that rose up.

"I know her sister Merry better. But we did hang out a few times. Man, those were wild parties."

How well did Trent know them? Esteban wasn't sure how he was going to ask his next question, but luckily Trent seemed to sense what was on his mind.

"I didn't sleep with either of them."

Esteban shouldn't care. Trent was happily married, and Esteban had no claim over June whatsoever, but he felt some of the tension leave his shoulders. "I've had it bad for June since high school. I didn't have the huevos to approach her about it until now."

"I wasn't wild enough for them," Trent continued. "They went for the bad boys and bronc busters."

"Yeah?" Esteban frowned. Shit, he had meant what he'd said to June tonight. He didn't have any secrets and he was boring. He had to make sure he didn't get too attached to her. She would be back on the circuit soon, but he didn't want to miss this opportunity to get to know her better.

*How can I expect to keep a girl like June interested?*

"Don't worry. Throwing down to defend your sister's honor is pretty badass."

"Are you reading my mind?" Esteban asked.

"Don't have to. You're asking the questions aloud."

*Maybe, I should slow down drinking.*

"If you want to be any good for your date tonight, I think that's a good idea."

# Chapter Six

WHEN JUNE SLIPPED behind the partition, she saw that the bachelorette party was already in high gear. The exotic dancers were well muscled, talented, and embarrassing the hell out of Emily.

Standing back, June took a couple of blackmail photos before getting in on the fun herself. Luckily, there was a lot of dancing to keep her mind off doing shots. June danced with April, her mother, Emily and Emily's sisters. She even did a shimmy number with a couple of the strippers, but she kept her clothes on this time—she had pushed her luck enough with public nakedness today.

"I can't believe you actually rode Athena naked down Main Street." Emily draped over her drunkenly. "Everyone in Last Stand is talking about you. And look at this turnout." Emily threw her hand wide across the party area. "I'd like to think they came here for me, but they probably came here to see what you would do next."

"That's not true," June said. "Everyone loves you here. They're all so excited about your wedding at the end of the month."

Times had been hard for the last year and a half. This

was the first big event that people were getting out of their houses and their comfort zones to attend. The COVID-19 pandemic had been devastating. It had destroyed lives, as well as livelihoods. But she wasn't going to think about that now. This was Emily's big night.

"I'm having so much fun," Emily said, giving her a noisy kiss on the cheek before being pulled back out to the dance area.

"I'm so glad," June said. She felt a little bit like an outsider, being the only one who was a hundred percent sober. Looking out into a group of women who'd obviously had more than a few drinks and were letting their inhibitions loose, she had a twinge that she was missing out.

*Since when do you need a drink to let your inhibitions loose?* a voice said in her head.

It had sounded so real that June actually looked around for her older sister. But Merry wasn't here tonight. And April was trying to stop their mother from stuffing dollar bills down the stripper's jockstrap. June flagged a waitress to get a refresher on her seltzer. While she was waiting, she texted Merry.

"Get a load of this." June sent a picture of their mother and April doing shots from an ice luge.

"I wish I was there," Merry texted back.

"Wish I wasn't sober," June replied.

"Don't start."

Immediately June felt bad. Merry had taken over all of June's responsibilities when she'd been sent to rehab. Merry was the last person she should be bitching to.

"I'm sorry," June typed. "R U coming to Emily's wedding?"

"That's the plan. Don't tell her in case of a last-minute emergency. I'll definitely be there, though, the week after for the Last Stand Rodeo.

"It will be good to see you. Things feel weird without you, and without being on the circuit."

"Well, you're not missing much. Shayna is still a bitch. Dustin is still hot, but looking a little miserable."

"Good." June wanted him to be miserable, at least for a little bit. If it hadn't been for him, she might very well still be on the circuit today.

No.

No one had polished off that half bottle of Jack Daniel's, but her. No one had forced her. It had been her choice. Of course, June had argued during her mandatory counseling sessions with Linda that she wouldn't have made that choice if she hadn't caught Shayna James giving her boyfriend a hand job. But part of rehab and getting her life straight was to admit that she made her own decisions. She sent Merry a few more pictures before heading back to dance. It was either that or get in on the tequila shots that were starting up in the back.

After a few hours, June had had enough. She had a low-grade headache from the music and strobe lights. Sick of running to the bathroom every twenty minutes, June laid off the seltzer. She wound up sitting with Kelly who was seven months pregnant. Kelly had been taking pictures all night. She was wearing a good game face, but June could tell the last place Kelly wanted to be was at Callum's at one in the morning with everyone dancing, drinking, and showing no signs of stopping.

June leaned in. "How about you and I blow this Popsicle stand and go get some hot fudge sundaes?"

"If I wasn't already married, I'd marry you." Kelly's eyes filled with tears.

"Don't start with the pregnancy hormonal bullshit," June said. "Otherwise, we're going to hit a twenty-four-hour drive-through for shakes, and then I'm dropping you off at the ranch."

"I promise, no tears."

Kelly and June made their way slowly up to Emily who was now sitting down with a bottle of rum and studying the karaoke playlist.

On the monitor set up by the stage, June could see that Mama was next in line waiting to sing "All My Exes Live in Texas," and April was in the queue for "Before He Cheats." June snorted. That should have been her song.

"Should I do 'Any Man of Mine' or 'Friends in Low Places'?" Emily asked.

"While the latter is true, the first one is more bridal."

"Shania it is," Emily said and scampered away to give her song choice to the DJ.

"June," her mother said, blocking her from following Emily. "What song are you going to sing?"

"The 'Na-Na-Na-Na-Hey-Hey-Hey-Goodbye' song."

"I love that song," her mother said, clutching at her arm and shaking it. "You know what would make this bachelorette party even better?"

"I can't imagine, but I've got a feeling you're going to tell me."

"Men," her mother said firmly and nodded her head.

"I think that's the whole point of a bachelorette party. No men allowed." June was very afraid her mother couldn't have fun without a man around. Maybe she should go to rehab for three months to figure out if she had as toxic a relationship with men as June apparently had with alcohol. But she didn't say that aloud because she didn't want to be a bitch, and the party was not a place to have that type of conversation.

"Your father was the best dancer," she said, swooning.

June snorted. "What are you talking about? He hated dancing because of his ingrown toenails."

"What?" her mother blinked drunkenly at her.

She gave her mom a quick hug. "Never mind, enjoy yourself."

Walking up to Emily and Kelly, June waited awkwardly while they hugged. Emily had glommed onto Kelly, telling her how much she loved her. It was really cute, but if June ever tried that crap with Merry, Merry would give her a titty twister or punch her in the gut.

Eventually, Kelly extracted herself and waved goodbye to the group. June gave Emily a quick hug, and then immediately spun her around and pointed Emily at the karaoke machine. "Your turn. Knock 'em dead." June swatted Emily on the butt, and then she hurried out with Kelly in tow.

The absolute quiet in the parking lot was a balm for her

sore ears.

"I really wish I had it in me to stay for karaoke," Kelly said. "But I'm ready to fall asleep. When did I become such a wimp?"

"Oh, I'd say about a child and a half ago."

"You're probably right. Doesn't mean you're not a bitch for saying it, though."

"Sorry," June said. "I'm feeling a little edgy."

"I was just teasing anyway. I get it. There's going to be a couple of other bridal party outings that won't be saturated in alcohol. We're all going to do a painting class together. It's going to be Texas bluebonnet landscape."

June didn't want to hurt Kelly's feelings by saying she'd rather stick the paintbrush up her nose than be sober and painting bluebonnets in a group, so she just nodded politely. June drove to a twenty-four-hour ice cream shop a couple towns over. The crowd was a little sketchy, so they took their hot fudge sundaes back to June's truck and ate them there.

"I love ice cream with chunks of stuff in it," June said, eating a spoonful of vanilla ice cream that was topped with chocolate syrup, a gummy bear, a pretzel and cookie crumbs.

"I like it all," Kelly said. "Or maybe I should say, the baby likes it all."

As they ate, June realized that she didn't have to wait for Emily to find out if Trent was hiring. She had Trent's wife in the truck with her right now.

"I was thinking that I might try my hand at teaching barrel racing to kids, now that I'm going to be in Last Stand for a while. Do you think Trent would be interested in hiring me on as an employee?"

"That's such a good idea. I don't see why not. I'll ask him. The only problem is we can't afford to pay you a salary. Things have been really tight lately, especially with my pregnancy forcing me to stay in bed some days. And enrollment has plummeted because of COVID. I'm sure we can work something out, though. Maybe you can take a percentage of the tuition for the students that you bring in?" Kelly asked.

That wasn't going to really help June with her bills right away. She'd have to find a job as soon as possible, but she didn't want to shoot herself in the foot because this could turn into a better opportunity, once things turned around a bit in the economy. "Yeah, maybe. Tell Trent I'll call him next week and maybe we can talk about it. But only if he's interested. I don't want to put him on the spot."

"Sounds like a plan," Kelly said. "I wish we could hire you on as his employee. I think you'd be great. And if you're planning on staying in Last Stand, this would be the perfect opportunity for you."

"I'm not sure if I am going to stay in Last Stand," June said, admitting it for the first time. "I think I need the excitement of a bigger city. Then again, I do really like it here. My family is here, and so are my friends. My real friends."

None of her rodeo friends had returned her calls. It was like they thought being fired was contagious. They were afraid they'd contract the disease if they talked to her. Or that Shayna would turn her beady little eyes on them and send her attack dog Sinclair to ruin their lives.

Not that June was bitter or anything.

Once she'd finished her ice cream, Kelly couldn't stop yawning.

"Let's get you home."

"I don't want to be so lame," Kelly said.

June knew the feeling. But since she wasn't pregnant, she decided to keep that comment to herself. She drove down the long driveway of the Three Sisters Ranch, past Trent's rodeo school, and turned the corner to the new house that Trent and Kelly had built. It was just past two, so she was surprised to see Trent and another man sitting on the porch.

"Oh, I hope they're not smoking cigars," Kelly said. "Otherwise, I'm going to throw up all over them."

"Why don't you stay here? I'll go check." June turned off the truck.

"Okay." Kelly nodded, leaning her head back on the seat and closing her eyes.

June walked up to the porch and was surprised to see Esteban sitting with Trent.

"You didn't call," he said.

"I just got free. I'm glad you're awake."

"I had something to look forward to." Esteban's smile charged her up and the restlessness burned away.

"How did you two meet?" Trent asked.

"This afternoon," Esteban said. "I was helping her out with some video she was shooting."

"Why didn't you ask Kelly?" Trent asked.

"It was a last-minute thing," June said.

"Is that my wife snoring in your truck?"

"She wasn't when I left her." June looked over and saw that Kelly's head was tipped back and her mouth was wide open. Now that she was listening for it, she could hear slight snores coming from her truck.

"She sent me ahead to make sure you hadn't been smoking," June said.

"I know better than that," Trent said. "We were just having a few beers and shooting the shit until it was time to go pick everyone up."

"The party's still going strong. We decided to cut out early," June said. "Do you want me to wake her?"

"No, don't bother. I got this." Trent walked over to the truck and opened the passenger's side door. He lifted his pregnant wife out and carried her up the stairs to the porch. "Thanks for bringing her home. I'm going to put us to bed. Have a nice night."

"Good night," June said, waving.

"I guess it's just you and me," Esteban said. "Buy you a drink?" He gestured to the cooler next to him. "There's soda."

"I'm going to explode if I drink anything more, but shouldn't we go someplace else?"

"We could," Esteban said. "But I'm a little too drunk to drive."

"I'll drive," June said. "We can go back to your place."

Esteban jerked his thumb behind him. "I live in a bunk-house with a bunch of other guys. There's no privacy."

"We can't go back to my mama's trailer. As soon as she

comes home, she'll burst into my room."

"And grab my ass?" he said.

"Probably. If we can't have sex, I want to do something wild," June said, whirling around in a circle.

"Why can't we have sex?" Esteban asked, with a cute frown.

"I suppose we could do it in my truck."

Esteban stretched to his feet and staggered slightly. "Whoa, did you feel the earth move?"

"I don't know. Why don't you kiss me again?"

He pulled her to him and kissed her. He tasted like whiskey and beer. Pressed up against him, she wanted to slow dance, even if there wasn't any music.

"You make my head spin," he whispered.

Holding his face between her hands, she said, "I'm good, but I think it's the alcohol that's doing that."

A cloud faded away from the moon and in the sudden light, she saw that he had a black eye.

"What the hell happened to you?" She had a moment of panic that he could have blacked out and not remembered what had happened.

"Got into a fight with my brother-in-law. He's a real piece of shit. If it wasn't for my niece, Dina, I'd snap his neck and throw him to the pigs." There was a slight slur in his voice.

"All right then, I think it's time I drove you home." Murder wasn't on her agenda for tonight, just in case he changed his mind.

"What about getting wild?" he asked, backing her up to

her truck.

On the other hand, she was pretty sure she could distract him into doing other fun things. "What about it?"

Grabbing her ankle, he encouraged her to wrap her legs around his waist. She was all for being taken on the hood of her truck—even on her maybe new boss's front lawn—but that would take a little more coordination than Esteban seemed to have in his grasp tonight. He kept slipping and she kept giggling, but it felt damned good.

"I'm sorry I drank so much," he said. "I wanted our date to be perfect."

"Don't apologize. Been there, done that, and got a three-month vacation from it. Do you have any water in that cooler over there?"

He nodded.

She slid off the hood and went to grab him one. Esteban opened the passenger door up and climbed into her truck. She got in too, and handed him the water. "You're going to want to drink this."

He did and then winced as he let his seat back.

"Are your ribs okay?" she asked. "Take off your shirt."

"I thought you'd never ask." Gingerly, he pulled the T-shirt over his head.

"That's a nasty bruise." June lightly touched the purpling mass on his side.

He hissed. "Ow, yeah. The son of a bitch hit me with a chair."

"I'll go get some ice." June took his T-shirt and went back to the cooler on the porch. She filled his T-shirt with ice and tied it off to create a makeshift ice pack.

Esteban's eyes were closed, but he jumped when she touched his ice-filled shirt to the bruise.

"Hold that there."

Grumbling, Esteban did. Wincing, he said, "It's cold."

"I can put the heat on, but if I start up the truck, I'm going to take you home."

"To the trailer and your ass-grabbing mother?"

"No, to the bunkhouse with the other men."

Esteban shifted so he could look at her. "I've got a better idea. A crazy idea."

"This doesn't involve feeding your brother-in-law to the pigs, does it?"

"Don't tempt me."

Pushing a lock of hair out of his eyes, June stroked his cheek. He nuzzled her palm. "What happened with your brother-in-law?"

"I'll tell you at the oasis."

"What's the oasis?" June said.

"It's a place where we can go skinny-dipping. Not that I'm trying to get you naked," he said hurriedly. "I'm not."

"Why not?"

"I'm not sure," he said slowly. "Could be because I can't do a lot about it."

"Don't worry. It doesn't take much to get me naked," June said. "We can try again tomorrow. So, tell me more about this oasis."

"That's what the ranch hands call this pond down in back of the Bullet pasture. The water is ice cold, even on a warm summer day. I can't imagine how cold it would be this time of night. Do you trust me?"

"Not to drown? I'm not sure. How drunk are you?"

"Too drunk to drive. Probably too drunk to swim. Sober enough to fool around in the truck for a bit."

"Let's go," June said. "Just tell me where to turn." After turning on the engine, she backed out of the driveway.

"You don't know me from Adam. How do you know I'm not going to take you out there for nefarious purposes and hide your body at the bottom of the pond?"

June giggled. "First of all, I like nefarious purposes and secondly you've already admitted to using pigs, not ponds, to dispose of bodies."

"I'd never hurt you," he said seriously.

"I know," June said.

"How?" He showed her his knuckles, which were torn up something fierce.

"You're not the type. You're the sweet boy next door."

"I'm not that sweet," he growled. "I drink. I gamble. I get into fights."

"I stand corrected. You are a bad boy. But I've known Kelly, Janice, and Emily for most of my life. If you were a bad seed, you wouldn't have made it up to being Nate's second-in-command."

"So you're saying that I've got good references."

"Yes, exactly."

He nodded. "I'm emotionally distant, according to Valerie."

"Fuck Valerie," June said.

"Yeah."

"Who's Valerie?"

"An ex who wanted me to leave Last Stand and take a job in Dallas with her."

"How long ago was this?"

Esteban leaned his head back on the seat. "Before COVID. I would have been stuck in quarantine with her."

"That would have been a test of your relationship. And I bet there wasn't a handy pen of pigs nearby."

"What did you do during quarantine when the rodeos weren't running?"

"Merry and I were in Australia when it hit. We stayed there until it was over. Mama and April were worried, but we had a blast."

Esteban gave her good directions and even in the cloudy night, on the barely there road, June was able to get to the oasis without bottoming out her truck or running off the path.

"This is it," he said.

June left her high beams on so it illuminated the area. "How deep is it?"

"It's about twelve feet at the center." He leaned in close to her and pointed out the rock face. "If it was daytime, we could climb up that and jump in."

There was a touch of cigar smoke around him, but it wasn't offensive—just a hint of spice, enough to be intriguing. It was a sweet smoky smell, and it made her want to rub her cheek against his.

"I'm dripping all over your seat," he said, hoarsely, dropping his T-shirt and the melted ice on the floor. Reaching for the water bottle, he drank half of it down. "I needed that. Thank you."

"Like I said, this is old hat for me."

"Am I disappointing you?" he asked.

"No. Never. But I am curious to hear about your fight with your brother-in-law."

"Cliff is a dick. He drinks too much, gambles too much, and is a shitty husband and father." Esteban blew out a frustrated breath. "But for some reason, Beatriz thinks he can do no wrong."

June nodded. It sounded like her mother. "Is he abusive?"

"No, because then…" He waved his hand.

"Pigs," June filled in.

"He keeps promising not to drink or gamble, but he does both and winds up breaking my sister's heart anyway. Worse, he just maxed out their credit cards at a chicken ranch in Nevada."

June winced. "I hope he got his money's worth."

"Tonight was just ugly, but it had been a long time coming. I caught him cheating on my sister. We fought. I got arrested."

"Highwater's having a busy day."

"He was off duty," Esteban said ruefully. "My brother-in-law is still there, as far as I know."

"Is your sister going to be all right?"

"Yeah, she's got an Uber scheduled to pick her up and bring her to Mama's house so she could be with Dina in the morning. She thinks Cliff's pulling a third shift, so at least she'll get to enjoy her night and morning before she finds out what happened tonight." Esteban blew out a big sigh. "I fucked up. I lost my temper and I think I made the situation worse."

"My sister is like you. Only she starts out swinging, whether there's alcohol or not. You seem the type to have a long fuse, but when it's time…kaboom!"

"Kaboom is right. I feel like such an idiot. I just want you to know, I'm not like this all the time. I've got to come clean. You had me pegged from the beginning. If you're looking for a bad boy, that's not me."

"Bad boys are overrated," she said. "I like cowboys with faded Levi's who can kiss."

Leaning in, she brushed her lips across his quickly, because she didn't want to hurt him if his mouth was sore from being used as a punching bag. He closed his eyes and tangled his fingers in her hair and kissed her more thoroughly.

Now that was what she was talking about. All thoughts of being bored, not being able to drink, and losing herself slipped away as she enjoyed his sweet kiss.

They never made it into the pond, but that was probably for the best because just when things were getting interesting, her phone started ringing. June wasn't sure how long they had been making out in the truck. Aside from Esteban being shirtless, the rest of their clothes were surprisingly still on. Normally when June went out with a guy, there were a few perfunctory kisses and then the clothes came off. After that, it was ride 'em cowgirl and get out fast before he wanted to cuddle, or worse, stay the night. But kissing Esteban was so damned good, she didn't want to stop to take her clothes off because then he might stop kissing her. And she never wanted the feeling of his lips on hers to end.

But the phone just wouldn't shut up.

"Are you going to answer that?" Esteban said, his voice husky and his eyes heated with desire. The call went to voicemail.

"Nope," she said and took advantage of the interruption to unbutton the front of her dress. This time Esteban nuzzled her collarbone and sank his teeth gently into the sweet juncture at the base of her neck. June's eyes rolled back in her head and her hand went for his belt.

Then her phone rang again.

"I can't believe this," June said.

Esteban kissed her lips firmly and then moved back in his seat. "You better answer it. Sounds like whoever it is, isn't going to give up."

"What?" June snapped into the phone.

Her mother's drunken voice came over the car speakers. "You need to come get me. April and Cole left hours ago. And I'm drunker than shit."

"Can't you get a ride home with Emily or somebody?"

"Donovan picked up Emily. And all those other losers went home before last call. If you're busy, I can see if there's a cowboy who's man enough to take me home." Her mother shouted that last bit away from the phone.

"No," June said. "I'll be right there. Don't go anywhere, especially not with a strange man." She hung up and put the car in gear. "I'm so sorry, but my mother is drunker than shit and I've got to pick her up."

"I heard," Esteban said.

June cursed her bad luck as she drove him back to the bunkhouse. "We have to do this again sometime, only with you sober."

Esteban grinned widely. "Name the time and place. I'm free any night but the bachelor party in a few weeks."

"What are you doing? Bunch of strippers at a titty bar?"

"No, it's poker night. Which is pretty much a monthly thing. Only this month will be a little bit different."

"Exotic dancers?"

"What's the difference between a stripper and an exotic dancer?"

"The hourly rate."

"No women allowed, but there might be fireworks."

"Fireworks sound like fun, but be careful. It's been so dry, you don't want to start a fire."

"Oh, not that type of fireworks," Esteban said. "Donovan's father, Charlie, is going to be there. And Donovan hates him."

"Then why is he going to his bachelor party?"

"Charlie has a knack of weaseling his way into things. Donovan and his father had a complicated relationship. Donovan changed his last name from Lincoln to Link and refused to speak to the man. Emily asked Donovan to give his father a chance. Donovan doesn't want to be alone with him, so he invited him to the next poker game. Unfortunately, Donovan didn't know we were throwing his bachelor party then."

"I hope having his estranged father there doesn't ruin his

night." She wasn't even sure she'd recognize her own father if he decided to show up on her doorstep one day.

"We won't let it. It's going to be awkward for the first couple hours, but once everyone smokes a few cigars and plays a hand or so of poker, it should be fine. I'm looking forward to going toe-to-toe with Charlie. From what I understand, he's a hell of a card player."

"Just don't play against Cole. You'll lose your shirt." Cole had been a professional poker player for many years, and still played in high-stakes games both locally and in Las Vegas.

"I already lost my shirt."

"It's on the floor."

"Right." Esteban stretched down to grab it. "Cole goes easy on us. But I think he's going to be dealing and not playing, so it's just the amateurs against each other."

"Too bad it's an all-male thing. I'd like try my hand against him."

"Maybe we can double date with him and April sometime."

"That sounds like fun." She parked outside the bunkhouse. "Honey, you're home."

"I'd invite you in, but your mother's drunker than shit."

"That she is. Another time," she said.

"Count on it." Esteban cupped her face in his hands and kissed her again. She felt that kiss straight down to her toes.

She watched until he was inside the bunkhouse before putting the truck into gear. She wasn't one for rebounds, but knew that if anyone could make her forget Dustin Greaves's betrayal, it was Esteban.

# *Chapter Seven*

MORNING WAS NOT Esteban's friend. When he staggered into the bathroom for an aspirin and a glass of water, he saw that his face and side looked like he'd been run over by a tractor. How had June not fled, screaming, from him last night? He had a brief moment of panic that he had dreamed up all their kisses in a beer-soaked fantasy. But then he checked June's social media, and he saw the pictures she had taken of the oasis earlier this morning. Apparently after she dropped her drunker than shit mother off, June came back to the Three Sisters Ranch and filmed herself jumping off the rock and into the water.

The camera was at a weird angle. It looked like she had propped it up on her truck's hood. It had still been dark out, and the lighting was bad from the headlights. The picture was fuzzy and vague. So while he couldn't make out individual body parts, he also didn't see any clothes.

Naked.

He liked that in a woman. Why had he gotten into a fight with Cliff and then got drunk? He didn't need alcohol when he could get drunk on June's kisses. What a ridiculous thought. He would've made fun of anyone else saying it.

God help him, now he was thinking girly stuff like that. After one day of being with June.

"Don't fall in love with her," he told his reflection.

Only his reflection knew that he'd had a crush on her for about five years, just from watching her compete. The fact that his fantasies might come true was enough to put a smile on his face.

He felt more human after a shower and a quick breakfast of toast and coffee. He didn't feel like making himself anything more than that. When Esteban had stalled long enough, he knew he had to go face the music. He needed to make sure Beatriz and Dina knew what they were walking into before Cliff made bail.

It was just past eight in the morning and most of the ranch hands were doing maintenance work in the several pastures around the large fifty-acre ranch. But Ringo and Frenchie were assigned chores around the farmhouse. Frenchie was taking care of the cattle that were in isolation because of suspected sicknesses, and Ringo was in the field, plowing. Nate was probably out with the rest of the team and Emily was still likely sleeping it off, so when the landline rang at the ranch house, he wasn't sure who could be calling. But he answered anyway.

"Three Sisters Ranch," Esteban said, hoping his voice didn't sound as hungover as he felt.

"When can Luis start?" Nate said without preamble.

"When do you want him?"

"Tomorrow works."

"He'll be here. Who do you want him to room with?"

"Bob."

"Done."

Nate hung up without a word about last night. It was possible he didn't know how bad Esteban had fucked up.

Esteban gave a fist pump, pleased that he hadn't ruined this opportunity for his brother. At least he could be the bearer of some good news. At this time of day, his brothers were probably still in bed, but it was time they got up. They had a lot of work to do to make sure Luis was ready to ride tomorrow morning around four a.m.

When he got to his mom's house, he walked in and stopped dead in his tracks when he saw Beatriz and Dina.

"*Tío* E, what happened to your face?" Dina ran up to him and he scooped her up into his arms. Beatriz met his look over Dina's shoulder, and her eyes filled with tears.

"An angry bull kicked me, but I showed him what's what. Why don't you go upstairs and wake up Tío L. I've got a surprise for him." With a kiss on her head, he set her down and she scampered up the stairs.

"Where's Mamá?" he asked when she was out of earshot.

"She's in the shower."

"Have you talked with Cliff this morning?"

"No, but I had several very interesting voicemail messages. The courthouse doesn't open for another hour. You want to tell me your side of it?" She put her hands on her hips and looked so much like their mother, he almost took a step back.

"I walked in on Cliff entertaining a lady friend in her underwear. I objected to that. We had a verbal disagreement.

I hit him. He hit me with a chair. And the police arrested us both. I made bail. I'm assuming he didn't."

"Not when his drug test came back positive for meth."

"Thank God."

"Not exactly my response," she said crossly.

Esteban closed his eyes in relief and was a little ashamed that he felt moisture at the corners.

"Benny?" Beatriz took his arm and led him into the kitchen. She hadn't called him that in years.

He sat down and rested his elbows on the table, sinking his eyes into his palms. After several shuddering breaths, he lifted up his head to look at her.

"He said he was going to divorce you and file for sole custody of Dina. He said he was going to kick you out of the house, because his name was on the lease, and the courts would agree to let her stay with him."

"Is that what he said?" She cocked her head at him. "Is that why you hit him?"

"No." Esteban hung his head in shame. "He said that because I hit him."

"Why did you hit him?"

Shaking his head, Esteban said, "He got to me. I should have known better, but he goaded me into it by saying unforgivable things about our family."

"And he hit you with a chair?"

Esteban pulled up his shirt and showed her his side. "The fight was pretty much over by then."

"Aiyee!" his mother screeched, coming into the kitchen. "Esteban, what happened to you?"

"I got thrown off my horse," he lied quickly, hoping his mother didn't remember he had two days off in a row.

"That place is too dangerous."

Esteban let her fuss over for him while Beatriz paced around the kitchen. He could tell she had more questions, but she didn't want to bring it up in front of their mother.

"What are you doing here so early, mijo?" she asked, smearing aloe vera on him wherever she could reach.

"Mamá, that stings."

"Don't be a baby," she chided.

"I have a surprise to tell you all," he said.

Alarmed, Beatriz shook her head, but he waved her off. "Not that," he mouthed over his mother's head.

"Well, what is it?" his mother asked.

"Luis! Sam! Get your asses down here," he yelled.

His mother jumped at the volume, and put a hand over her heart. "Esteban, language."

Sam and Luis groggily stumbled down the stairs in their boxer shorts, swinging Dina between them.

"Not on the stairs," Beatriz said, but they didn't listen to her.

"Did you put ice on these?" Mamá asked as everyone clambered into their seats around the table. "How's your eyesight? Can you see?"

"I'm fine," he said.

"How about bacon, eggs and pancakes for breakfast?"

"Nope, were all going out to eat for breakfast. My treat."

"Yay!" Dina said.

"Why do we have to go out to eat? I've got everything for

breakfast here," his mother said.

"What happened to your face?" Sam asked.

"He got thrown by his horse at that awful place," his mother said.

"Because we're celebrating," Esteban said, answering his mother's first question.

"You got a girlfriend?" she asked, delightedly clutching his arm.

"Not yet, but I'm working on it." Esteban wasn't ready to have that conversation with his mother. He'd wait until he and June dated for a bit before he tossed that grenade into the kitchen. *Remember the naked girl on the horse...?* "Now, the good news is that Nate wants Luis to start work tomorrow on the ranch."

His mother seemed more excited about that announcement than his two brothers.

"Why not me?" Sam asked, rubbing his eyes, still barely awake.

Esteban wasn't quite sure how to answer that, especially with his mother in the room, so he just said, "We went in alphabetical order."

Sam nodded and said to his mother, "Why couldn't you have named me Adam?"

"Don't worry," his mother said. "It's just a matter of time before you get your turn, right?"

"Yeah," Esteban said. It made perfect sense. They needed another few men so that they could have a shift that worked out in the fields, a shift that worked in the pastures, and a shift that rotated doing the daily chores around the ranch and for emergency purposes. At full capacity, the bunkhouse had room for twelve men. Right now, they were stretched thin. It had been that way for the past year. But things were starting to get better. His mother was right. It was only a matter of time before another job opening on the ranch came up. And Sam was a shoo-in. "As long as Luis doesn't fuck things up."

"Esteban, language." This time she smacked him when Dina giggled.

"Sorry, Mamá. That's not a word I want to hear from you," he said, pointing at Dina.

"What time do I start?" Luis asked. "Do I get my own room?"

"Four a.m. and no, you don't get your own room. So after breakfast, we're going to come back here and we'll pack up your things and move you into the bunkhouse. You'll be rooming with Bob."

While the boys went back upstairs to get ready, his mother said, "This means so much to me, that you did this for your brother."

"I told you, Mamá, it was just a matter of being patient."

"I get so worried about you boys." She dabbed her eyes.

He hugged her and was astounded at how frail she seemed. She always seemed to be made of iron and full of piss and vinegar. But lately, she had been slowing down and had been letting her worries get the best of her.

"Now all we need is for you to get Sam a job, too. If he has to live in the bunkhouse, I won't have to worry about him living in sin with Anne."

And there was the iron will. Comforted, instead of annoyed, Esteban said, "Go on and get ready. I'll make sure the boys stay on track and get dressed."

"Good luck with that," she muttered as she went upstairs.

"Hey, peanut," Esteban said. "Do you want to play games on my phone?"

"Yeah!" Dina scrambled up and grabbed it from him, her fingers tapping furiously.

"Just stay away from the casino games," he said, taking Beatriz by the arm so they could talk in the backyard without being interrupted.

"I don't want to get divorced," Beatriz said, sitting down on the back step.

"You want to stay with that asshole?" Esteban scowled.

"No, I want to do like Mamá did and just never see him again."

"What if you meet someone else?"

Beatriz snorted. "I doubt that."

"He's already met a few people. Leeches like him want to glom on to the next victim. I think he meant what he said about kicking you out and keeping Dina. I think we should do a pre-emptive strike and move you and Dina out first. Once she's settled here at Mamá's, the court isn't going to want to upset her by having her move back in with him, especially if he's got a drug charge."

"If I leave him, my marriage is over."

"Bea, your marriage was over when he maxed out your credit cards in Nevada."

"Don't you think I know that?" she snapped. Rubbing the back of her hand across her eyes, she said, "What am I going to tell Dina? What am I going to tell Mamá?"

"The truth, watered down for Dina."

"Mamá is going to be devastated. You know how she is about the sanctity of marriage."

"She's just going to have to get over it. With Luis and soon Sam bunking at the Three Sisters Ranch, Dina can stay in their room and you can have your old bedroom back."

"Just what I always wanted. To be a thirty-year-old single mom living in her mother's sewing room."

"Better than being miserable in a marriage with a drunk drug addict who likes to gamble and sleep with whores."

"When you put it like that…" Beatriz sighed. "I wish I believed he wanted to change."

"He doesn't."

She stood up and hugged him. "Stay away from him. I don't want him to hurt you again."

"He needs to stay away from me. I owe him for that chair."

"I mean it, Benny. He can be vindictive."

"I noticed," Esteban said dryly.

They walked back in and Dina said, "Who's June?"

"Why?" Esteban said.

Dina held up his phone. "She said she had a great time last night and can't wait to see you again."

"Give me that." Esteban blanched and snatched his phone back. Who knew what else June might send? He eagerly searched for any pictures, but there weren't any.

"Dina, you know better than to read other people's messages," Beatriz scolded.

"I couldn't help it. It buzzed and then the words flashed up."

Esteban was glad that June hadn't gotten into more graphic detail. "Soon," he texted back. He wanted to make sure his sister and brother were settled before he made any plans. But he couldn't stop grinning.

"So who's June?"

"June Grayson is a tart," his mother said, coming back downstairs.

"Mamá," Esteban said. "She's just extroverted."

"She's trouble."

"Yeah," he said, still grinning.

"Why are we talking about June?" his mother asked.

"No reason." Esteban stuffed his phone in his back pocket.

"She had a great time with Tío last night and wants to do it again," Dina said.

"Dina," Beatriz scolded, but it would have been more believable if she wasn't laughing.

"Esteban, I don't want you seeing that loose woman," his mother said.

"I'm not discussing this with any of you right now. I'm going to check on the boys."

Feeling like he had dodged a bullet, Esteban went upstairs and pushed the door open to his old room. Luis was on his phone and Sam had gone back to bed.

"If you're not downstairs and ready to go in five minutes,

we're leaving without you and you can fend for yourself for breakfast. While we're gone, Sam better help you pack."

"I was just resting my eyes for a second," Sam said, getting out of bed and hurrying to the bathroom before his brother could get there.

"Don't use all the hot water," Luis said, pounding on the closed bathroom door.

"I think Mamá already beat you to that," Esteban said. He sat down on the bed that used to be his, which the twins had made into a couch so that they could sit and play video games in their room.

"Beatriz is moving back home with Dina."

Luis looked up from his phone. "Did he hurt them?"

"Not physically. It's the same old shit."

"Did he hurt you?"

"He tried. He's in jail right now, waiting for bail. He'll probably get out later today. I think we should move Beatriz and Dina before we move you."

"Yeah, okay. Does Mom know yet?"

Esteban shook his head. "Beatriz should be the one to tell her. She might be doing that now."

"I'll help and if Cliff tries to stop us, he can see how he likes fighting with me. You may have taken boxing, but I went for mixed martial arts. He won't touch me."

"The fucker is fast and he fights dirty," Esteban said sourly.

"So do I." Luis cracked his knuckles.

"Let's just concentrate on getting everyone moved around. Do you know what you want to take to the ranch?"

"I don't have all that much. I'll leave the PlayStation here and Sam can bring it when he gets the job. Do you think they'll let us room together?"

Esteban shrugged. "That's between you and the other guys. I don't see why not. But you might want to try living with someone else for a change."

"It's going to be weird, not being here."

"Are you sure this is something you want to do?" Esteban asked. "Because it's not too late to give the job to Sam, if this isn't what you're looking for."

Luis put his phone away and pulled out a battered suitcase from under his bed. "I need a job. I need to get out of this house. Being a ranch hand at the Three Sisters Ranch fulfils both those things."

"Good enough." Esteban tugged Sam's suitcase out from under his bed so they could use that as well. Sam wasn't going to be using it for a few weeks at least. It would make moving Luis into the bunkhouse easier if half his gear wasn't in garbage bags.

"I'll work hard," Luis said.

"I know you will."

Sam came out of the bathroom wearing just a towel. "Next."

"I'm going to check and see how things are going downstairs," Esteban said. "Hurry up and get dressed."

Downstairs, Dina was watching a Marvel movie and he smelled bacon coming from the kitchen. Confused, he followed his nose. His mother was scrambling up enough eggs to feed an army and Beatriz was quietly sobbing at the kitchen table.

"What happened?" he asked, warily.

"We're eating here. And then we're going to pack up Dina and Beatriz's things and bring them here. I'll stay here with Dina and clear out the sewing room."

"Have one of the boys stay too, to help you with the heavy lifting," Esteban said, not wanting to argue when his mother was barely holding herself together. Her hand shook on the whisk as tears poured down her face. He couldn't tell if she was mad or sad.

"Did he do that to your face?" she asked.

Esteban looked at Beatriz, but she was still crying silently into a wad of tissues.

"Don't lie to me," his mother said vehemently.

"Yes," he said reluctantly. "But I started the fistfight."

Her mouth thinned into a bloodless line. "I wanted this to work out. I had hoped counseling would help."

"He didn't want to be helped," Esteban said.

"Marriage is forever," she said. "But if he could do that to you…" His mother poured the eggs into the large skillet. "If he ever hit the baby, I'd never forgive myself."

Esteban didn't know what to say. If Cliff ever hit Dina, there wouldn't be enough bail to keep Esteban out of jail. "I think divorce is the best option."

"It's not," his mother said. "But if it keeps Dina safe, I can understand it."

"It's good for Beatriz too," Esteban said, trying not to get steamed.

His mother didn't say anything. Instead, she reached for

the tortillas and started warming them up in the oven.

"Do you want me to go over there and wait for you guys?" Esteban asked Beatriz.

"No," his mother said. "You don't go there without her and your brother. I don't want Cliff making up any stories about you robbing him or anything."

Esteban decided the best thing they could all do was eat what she cooked and then do exactly what she said. He got his sister a cup of coffee. Squatting down next to her, Esteban asked, "Is there anything you need?"

She shook her head. "You're doing it."

When they all sat down at the table, Beatriz told Dina that they were going to move out of their house and come stay with *abuela*.

"Is Daddy coming?" she asked.

"No, honey. Daddy and I are getting a divorce."

Dina's face crumbled and Esteban's heart just about tore in two. He wished she had dropped that bomb a little more gently, but he guessed it was like ripping off a Band-Aid.

"Why?"

Beatriz swallowed hard. "Mommy and Daddy love you very much. That's not going to change. But we don't... We can't..." She floundered and looked at Esteban for help.

His mother was stoically shoveling eggs into her mouth and the twins were concentrating on their breakfast burritos.

"Sometimes adults just grow apart," Esteban said, jumping in. "This has nothing to do with you."

"That's right," Beatriz said. "This is between Mommy and Daddy. Your abuela and tíos—all of us love you very much."

"Everything is going to change, isn't it?" Dina wailed.

"Not everything," Beatriz said. "You'll still go to Last Stand Elementary School. You'll still see all your friends. We'll just be living here."

"School is almost out, though. Are we still going to plant our garden?"

Beatriz winced. "Not at the house, but we can do that here."

"Daddy promised I can do barrel racing this summer."

"Absolutely not," his mother said.

"We can't afford lessons or the gear," Beatriz said, soothingly.

"He said you would say that." Dina scowled and tossed down her fork.

Esteban jumped into the conversation, his mouth moving faster than his brain. "I have a friend who can help. I bet she'll do it for free."

Beatriz raised an eyebrow at him.

"No," his mother said. "It's too dangerous. It's not right. Girls should not be on horses riding at breakneck speed."

"Daddy will let me." Dina pouted.

"But here's the thing," Esteban said, leaning toward Dina. "This is going to be hard enough on your mommy and daddy without you playing one of them off against the other."

"Benny," Beatriz said. "She's too young to be manipulative like that."

"Doesn't matter." Esteban leaned back in his chair. "Do

you know who June Grayson is?"

His mother scraped back her chair and noisily tossed her plate into the sink and ran water.

Dina snorted. "Duh, everyone knows June Grayson."

Esteban placed his phone on the table and looked at his niece. She stared at him like he was an idiot and then comprehension flitted over her face.

"June. That June?"

He nodded.

"You're going to get June Grayson to teach me how to barrel ride?" Dina leapt up from her chair and started dancing around. "You're the best tío ever."

"Hey," his brothers said in unison with their mouths full.

"Esteban, I don't know about this," Beatriz said.

"We'll do it at Trent's, after hours," he said.

Beatriz looked at her mother's stiff back. "If you're sure…"

"Oh thank you, Mommy." Dina wrapped her arms around Beatriz's neck.

"But you have to keep up your end of the deal," Esteban said, pointing at Dina. "If Mom says no and Dad says yes, that's between the two of them to decide who's right. You stay out of it. Promise?"

"Pinkie promise?" Dina held up her pinkie.

"I don't…" he looked at his sister for help, but she just smiled at him "…know what that is."

Dina sighed in exasperation. "A pinkie promise is absolutely unbreakable. It's the strongest thing there is. You can't break a pinkie promise or bad stuff happens."

"Well, we don't want that." Esteban shook her pinkie.

"No," she groaned. "Like this." She looped her pinkie around his and gave a tug.

"I'm glad that's settled," he said.

Now, he just had to hope that June wouldn't mind giving a few lessons for free. How did he get himself into these things? Oh right, his mouth engaged before his brain caught up.

# Chapter Eight

I T HAD BEEN a couple of days since she had seen Esteban, and June was beginning to feel like he just wasn't into her. She supposed that was for the best. Esteban wasn't like the men she was used to dating. Still, she found herself thinking about those endless kisses in her truck.

So when he rang her up out of the blue and wanted her to meet him at Trent's rodeo school for lunch, she was pleasantly surprised. He was waiting for her by the barn when she got there.

"I brought a picnic lunch," he said, when he saw her. "I can't be gone too long, but I wanted to spend some time together and ask a favor."

She had been wondering if there was a catch. Was this a nice way of blowing her off and telling her he didn't want to see her again? He didn't need to go to all this trouble. Instead of taking the horses, they took his truck. Laughing, she recognized they were going to the oasis when they made the turn by the now-familiar dirt road.

"Are we going to go skinny-dipping?"

"Unfortunately, no. I've got an hour and then I've got to get back to work. If I'm not back in time, it's my ass."

"Okay, I won't tempt you." But June was disappointed. She wasn't used to waiting for a man she wanted.

The disappointment quickly fled when she realized that he brought over some of Sarah Sullivan's fried chicken and potato salad. They sat next to each other, enjoying the shade as they ate lunch. "So, what's the favor?" June asked, wiping her greasy fingers and mouth on a wet wipe once she had demolished the food on her plate. She sat back with a bottle of root beer and wondered what Esteban had in mind.

"Remember my brother-in-law?" Esteban pointed to his black eye, that looked a million times better, but the bruise was still there.

"I'm not helping you cut up the body for the pigs."

"You don't need to cut up a body, just throw it in the pen."

"I just ate," June said, holding her hand to her stomach.

"Sorry. Anyway, he and my sister are getting a divorce."

"I'm sorry to hear that." It didn't surprise her—most marriages ended up that way. But she knew from experience it was rough.

"It's for the best. He's an asshole, but his daughter loves him."

June winced. "How old is she?"

"Dina is seven years old."

The same age June was when her parents got divorced.

"He promised that this summer, he'd get her barrel-racing lessons. Only there's no money. There never was. It was destined to be a disappointment the moment he said it. Only now, there's the pain of the separation and the divorce.

My sister and niece are living with my mother."

"And you want me to give your niece some private lessons?" What a sweet man he was to take time out of his busy day to try and help a little girl who was hurting. June felt her shriveled heart melt a bit.

"It doesn't have to be private," he said. "I talked to Trent and he thinks adding you to his roster is a great idea."

"Wait, you talked to Trent about him hiring me on as an instructor?" She had been putting off that conversation because she didn't want to face the fact that Trent might not want a wild Grayson sister teaching at his school.

"Did I overstep? If you don't want to, it's all right. I just figured you might want something to keep you occupied until you're ready to go back to the rodeo."

"Esteban, if you didn't have to go back to work, I'd kiss you. And I think you and I both know where that kiss would lead to."

"I've been thinking about nothing else this week," he said.

"Then why haven't we gotten together? I'm wearing out the batteries in my vibrator."

June watched as he swallowed wrong and choked on his soda.

"You're trying to kill me."

"I'm trying to get you into bed."

"I'm there," he said.

"Unfortunately, we have a logistics problem. Specifically, my mother and your roommates."

"Yeah, I might be able to sneak you past one or two, but

someone is going to see you."

"Esteban, someone would hear me."

He closed his eyes and groaned. "We could get a hotel," he suggested. "I don't have another day off to enjoy it though until next week. My days off this month are going to be blown on the bachelor party and the wedding."

She straightened up. "Do you want to be my date for the wedding?"

"Yes," he said.

"Good. I've got a room at the hotel where the ceremony is taking place. We can sneak back and have a couple of quickies during the reception and then spend the night together."

"You want to wait until the end of the month to have sex?"

"No. But do you have a better idea?"

"I don't," he said. "Still, I want to see you before then."

"Good because I'm not going to this painting thing without you."

"Painting thing?" he asked.

"It's tomorrow night. You're my date. I'll give you the details later." She started packing up the picnic. "You've got to get back, and I've got some things to hammer out with Trent."

"Hey," he said as they were about to get back into the truck. He slung his arm around her and pulled her close. "You don't have to teach at Trent's school, if you don't want to. I'm not trying to pressure you."

"I'd love to help your niece and I'd love to work with

Trent." June cupped Esteban's face in his hands and kissed him hard, putting all her joy and excitement into it. He pressed her back against the truck and rocked his hips between her thighs. Wrapping her arms around his neck, she wished they had more time.

His watch alarm interrupted them this time and again, June came up for breath wondering how much time had passed.

"I want you," he whispered and nipped at her neck.

"Find the time and the place before the wedding and you can have me," she said.

"I'm on it." He winced as he adjusted himself.

Trailing a hand over the hard bulge in his jeans, June nuzzled his cheek.

"You're not helping and I'm going to be late," he said, but there wasn't a lot of protest in his voice.

"Fine," she sighed in fake aggravation. Looked like she'd be stopping at the drug store for more batteries on the way home.

Esteban dropped her off in front of the school and sped off back to work. She itched to go get Athena and take her around the barrels, but the classes that were going on were bull-riding related. She hoisted herself up on the fence and watched until the students recognized her and then it was too much of a distraction. With an apologetic look at Cole, she hopped the fence and walked over to talk to the kids.

"I see you know who this is," Cole said to them. "This is my future sister-in-law."

"You're marrying Merry?" one of the older boys said,

shocked and impressed.

June snickered. "No, he's marrying my other sister— April."

"Does she do rodeo?"

"No, she does taxes," June said. "A much better life skill. So, show me what Cole has been teaching you."

The boys demonstrated how to fall correctly, and then begged her to come inside and watch them on the bull-riding machines. She did, marveling at how nice the school was. June wished something like this had existed when she was growing up, not that Mama could have afforded to pay for it.

Midway through the indoor lesson, Trent came out of his office. She saw out of the corner of her eye that he was limping.

"Have you talked to Esteban?" he asked.

"Yeah," she said.

"Do you have a minute?"

"I do." She waited until the kids were distracted and then joined Trent in his office.

"Have a seat," he said, closing the door behind them.

"How's the knee?" she asked as he sank into his chair.

"It's going to rain like hell. My knee is a barometer now."

"That sucks." She had seen that bull ravage Trent the first time it happened. The fact that he'd got on it a second time proved he had more *cojones* than most men she knew.

"I've got some bad news and it sucks," he said.

"Hit me with it." June appreciated his upfront manner.

She was a big girl. She could take rejection as long as he didn't sugar-coat it.

"I can't hire you on officially as an instructor." ·

Official didn't mean squat to her. "Is this a money thing? Because Kelly already explained that we might have to work out a commission payment scale."

Trent shook his head. "I'm not sure how the WPRC found out that I was considering hiring you, but they sent me an offer I can't refuse if I don't hire you."

"What are you talking about?" June asked, confused.

"I got a call today from Sinclair Thompson."

June's fists clenched. "What did that asshole want?"

"He said that if I didn't hire you, they would pay an instructor to teach at my school for the summer and give my school a bunch of free advertising at the Texas events."

"Holy crap," June said. "That's a shitload of money they just flung at you."

"June, who the hell did you piss off over there?"

That was a good question. June told him the Shayna James saga that ended up with her in rehab and with Shayna's new hairdo.

Trent whistled. "You should have shaved her bald. I wish with all my heart that I could tell them to stick it up their ass. But after last year, the free advertising and free instructor they're offering are just the thing that will help me get the school back in the black."

"I don't blame you," June said, shaking her head. Whoever was behind this was brilliant. If they had low-balled Trent, he would have refused the deal. They literally made him an offer he couldn't refuse.

"I feel terrible about this," he said. "And Kelly's not talking to me."

"I'll fix it with Kelly. This is a no-brainer. You had to take their deal."

"But," he said. "Unofficially, if you want to take in some students after hours, I'll look the other way."

"I appreciate that," she said. "But I don't want to jeopardize your sweet deal." It hurt. It hurt, as if Shayna was kicking her in the ribs all over again. And she had no doubt that when she asked Merry to dig around, they'd find Shayna's fake nails and bleached-blond hairs all over this.

Forcing herself to get to her feet, she said, "There are no hard feelings, Trent. I mean that sincerely, and I'm happy that this deal is going to bring you some money."

"I can't tell you what a relief it is to hear you say that. And the minute they're off my neck, if you want a job, you've got it." He shook her hand. "You're the best barrel racer I've ever seen."

"I won't tell Merry you said that."

"I'd appreciate that." Trent walked her out, his limp even more pronounced, but she knew enough stubborn men not to suggest he sit down and rest it.

"I do have one request," she said.

"Name it," he said.

"Can you make sure that Esteban's niece doesn't have to pay tuition?"

"Already had that idea. No worries."

"Good," June said. At least that little girl would have

something to concentrate on instead of her parents' failing marriage. Lord knew that barrel racing had gotten her and Merry through those rough patches.

Marriage just sucked.

So did life.

But mostly Shayna James and Sinclair Thompson sucked.

Shayna had pretty much dominated the last couple events. Merry was literally the only thing standing in the way of Shayna winning the hefty purse for the WPRC barrel-racing championship.

June should probably go to Merry and help watch her ass. It was only a matter of time before Shayna decided to sabotage her, too. And it wasn't as if June had anything else to do.

The thing she couldn't figure out was why Sinclair was backing Shayna so hard. If he was betting on her, he'd have better luck putting his money on June or Merry. If Shayna was sleeping with him to get to the top, that didn't make sense, either. There were higher ranking officials in the WPRC.

Shaking her head, June drove back to the farmhouse to check on Kelly and ask her to let Trent off the hook.

"I'm sorry, June, but she's out like a light. She doesn't sleep much these days, so I don't want to wake her," Sarah Sullivan said when June walked up to the farmhouse. She was unpacking the dirty dishes from the chuck wagon, so June helped her clean it out.

"There she is," Frank Sullivan said, holding out his arms.

"The best damn barrel rider in all of Texas."

"I keep hearing that," June said and welcomed the strong hug. She definitely needed one.

"I want to see you back on the circuit," he said, wagging his finger at her.

"That's not up to me," she said.

Frank narrowed his eyes. "That don't sound like the June I know."

It didn't, did it?

"I'll get back there sooner or later," she said. And just saying that aloud made her feel a little better.

"I got to check on the calves. You think about what I said." Emily's father grabbed his hat and walked out of the ranch house.

Sarah sighed. "Don't mind him. He's a big fanboy for rodeo."

"I remember," June said with a smile. "Thanks for the picnic lunch you packed for me and Esteban."

"I didn't have anything to do with that," Sarah said, but she flushed with pleasure.

"Of course, you did. There were cloth napkins and wet wipes. It's the little touches that gave you away."

"Well, I'm glad the two of you enjoyed it. He's a nice young man."

"I like him," June said.

"He's over the moon about you," Sarah said.

June felt the same way after only a few kisses. She wondered if she should be running the other way instead of running into bed with him.

"I think Emily is over at the hunting lodge with Donovan, if you want to say hello," Sarah said when they finished with the chuck wagon.

"I haven't seen her since the bachelorette party," June said.

"Wasn't that fun? I can't wait for the painting party."

"Yeah," June said, lying through her teeth. "Me, too." At least Esteban would be with her so she didn't feel like a big loser when all the couples were giggling over their masterpieces and drinking wine.

After heading to the barn first, June took care of Athena, giving her a nice brushing and special treatment before saddling her up. Maybe she could convince Emily to set up one of the empty pastures as a barrel-racing training ground. If Janice could have a dressage ring back here, why not a place for a real horse event? She'd have to float that by Janice just to see the look on her face. Actually, that gave June an idea.

June went in search of Janice. She found her doing some gardening by the retreat center.

"Hey, how's it going?" June said.

"Good." Janice wiped her arm across her face, leaving a trail of dirt.

"I've got a favor to ask."

"Name it."

"Can I spend the night at the retreat center tomorrow night after the painting party?"

"Sure, why?"

June smiled. "Can you keep a secret?"

"Not even remotely."

"Fair enough. Esteban and I have been having a little trouble connecting since I live with my mom and he lives with a bunch of other guys."

Janice held up her hand. "Say no more. I'll make up a room for you guys. Just toss the sheets in the washer in the basement before you leave in the morning."

"You're the best," June said.

"Esteban Lopez, huh." Janice smiled. "He doesn't seem your type."

"He's not. I think that's why I like him so much."

"Just be careful with him. Guys like that tend to get involved quickly. I wouldn't want to see him hurt."

June tried not to get miffed, but with her reputation, she guessed it wasn't out of line. "I'll be extra careful with him."

"Well, not too careful." Janice grinned and went back to her flowers.

June's next stop was the hunting lodge, but she only got halfway there when she saw Emily heading toward her on her horse, Sunflower.

"You look like someone shot your dog," Emily said when they were alongside each other.

"I don't even have a dog to shoot," June said and told her about the latest bullshit.

"I think we need to get Merry involved," Emily said. "She will cut the bitch."

"I know. And I might mention it to her at the wedding. But not before. She's got two big events that she needs to crush Shayna in. I don't want her distracted."

"This is so damned unfair to you. Blacklisting you on the circuit was bad enough, but now Shayna James is going after your livelihood."

"I'm not sure it's her, because I didn't think she had that kind of money or influence."

"Maybe she's got her hand down this Sinclair Thompson's pants, too."

"Hmmm." That gave June an idea.

"Hmmm?" Emily prodded.

"What if that's true? She's getting married to Dustin. I bet if we put our minds to it, we could catch Shayna and Sinclair in the act. Then we could blackmail her into backing off."

"Except blackmail is illegal," Emily added.

"What she's doing to me should be illegal. Do you think Kelly is up for some fun?"

"You are not dragging my pregnant sister all over Texas to try and catch Shayna James cheating on your ex-boyfriend."

"Fine, I'll go myself. It's not as if I'm doing anything anyway. I just figured since she was the camera expert, I'd ask her."

"This sounds like a caper," Emily said.

"It's definitely a caper. But it's going to require a road trip."

"That's all you had to say. If I don't get away from here for a few days, I'm going to go insane."

"I need you to do some research on Sinclair Thompson. Call him up and see if you can get some information about his schedule. Pretend that you're interested in sponsoring an event or something. In the meantime, I'll see what I can dig up on Dustin and Shayna's whereabouts. Ideally, we'll be able to pinpoint a spot where Shayna and Sinclair will be together and then we'll get out the cameras."

"Are you sure we won't get into trouble?" Emily asked.

"I'm banned from competing, not from attending WPRC functions. And I know just the cowgirl who can give us passes to go behind the scenes."

June let Athena lead them back to the barn on her own while she searched online for Dustin and Shayna's schedules.

"Got 'em," she said triumphantly.

"I'm still gathering information on this Sinclair douche." Emily flashed her a picture. "Doesn't he look like he should have 'buy a used car from me' under his picture?"

June nodded. "He's definitely a weasel."

"He's never been married, that I can find. But he has a reputation for being a ladies' man."

"I never saw him sniffing around the arenas," June said.

"He goes after the women in the audience mostly, from what I can pull from Facebook. I don't think he's banging Shayna."

"That's too bad," June scowled. "Maybe her mother?"

"I'll see if there are any rumors or inuendoes," Emily said, tapping away. "What did you find?"

"Shayna and Dustin are doing a meet-and-greet event in Fort Worth tonight. Sinclair is going to be there as well, to take care of the promotions. So that's where we need to be. I bet it won't be hard to catch them in some kind of shenanigans."

"That's a long drive," Emily said. "And we have the painting party at Janice's tomorrow with the rest of the bridal party."

"I can do this alone," June said.

"No." Emily shook her head. "I'm in. You just have to promise me that we'll be back here in time for the party tomorrow."

"We will," June said. And maybe she and Esteban would have something to celebrate in their private room after the painting was done.

# Chapter Nine

JUNE LOVED THE Fort Worth Stockyards. She grabbed a bag of popcorn and walked with it down the line of shops. The doors to the rodeo opened at six, but Dustin and Shayna were outside taking pictures with the fans.

Emily showed her the picture of Sinclair Thompson on her phone again. "Keep your eye out for this douche. He's your target, not the queen bitch and her consort."

June knew Emily was right. "We should split up. I'll take the left-hand side of the street, you take the right. If you see him, stay on him and give me a call. I'll do the same."

"You got it." Emily stalked across the street, but June couldn't bring herself to move just yet. She wished that Merry was at this event. She wanted to see her sister with her own eyes and make sure she was holding up despite the pressure of competition. Shayna kept looking at her watch and drinking from a frosted tumbler. From experience, June knew that it had vodka and diet cranberry juice. Back then, June's had been Jack and Diet Coke. Merry had stuck to water.

Leaning up against the building, June watched Shayna fake smile to the crowd. Her face had to hurt after a while.

Dustin must have ducked inside to take a break because she didn't see him, until she turned around to finally start looking for Sinclair, and nearly ran face first into him.

"What are you doing here?" Dustin asked warily.

"I need to talk to Sinclair Thompson," she said, deciding to brazen it out. "Do you know where I can find him?"

"He's inside talking to the announcers. Come on back." He inclined his head.

June shot a quick text to Emily: "Dustin is taking me to Sinclair. Keep an eye on Shayna."

"You look good," Dustin said.

"So do you." This was really weird. He was acting normal. Didn't he realize nothing was normal anymore?

"I didn't see you on the roster. Are you a last-minute replacement?" he asked.

Narrowing her eyes at him, she couldn't figure out his angle. But he was leading her past security and into the arena where she could talk with Sinclair, so she was willing to play his game.

"Sinclair's been involved with some new business ventures of mine." Sabotaging them, but Dustin didn't need to know about that.

"Cool," he said. "Hey, I know it's been a while and I don't blame you if you're still pissed at me, but I'm sorry about how it all went down with Shayna."

Taken aback at the apology, June wasn't sure how to respond.

"Dustin, June, over here," one of the backstage people said, holding up a cell phone.

It was second nature to turn to the camera and smile. She hadn't realized Dustin's arm was around her until after the flash.

"Get off me." She pushed him.

"Where have you been?" he asked.

"Seriously?" But then she looked into his eyes. He had pale blue eyes that she used to find dreamy. Now she just found them vacant. He wasn't smart enough to play dumb.

"I took a sabbatical," she said. How did he not know Shayna beat her up and June went to rehab?

"And now you're back."

"No, she's not," Shayna said, wrenching Dustin away from June.

*Thanks for the heads-up, Emily.*

"She said she's here to talk to Sinclair."

"Sinclair doesn't want to talk to her," Shayna said, wrapping herself around Dustin.

June was relieved that she couldn't care less. All it did was make her wish Esteban was here with her, which should have alarmed the hell out of her, but it didn't.

"How do you know?" June asked.

"You're no longer a part of professional rodeo. You're a has-been. You have no place here promoting a sport that doesn't want you," Shayna said.

"Harsh," Dustin chastised.

"June, over here."

With a triumphant look at Shayna, June turned with a flourish and mugged for several camera shots as the people that had been allowed behind the scenes started to gather around the three of them.

"Are you riding tonight, June?" one of them asked.

"Where have you been?" another said.

Two reporters started closing in. Out of the corner of her eye, she saw Sinclair Thompson hurrying over to intercept them.

"Can't talk now, guys." With a wave, she met him half-way.

"You're trespassing," he gritted out through a smile.

"I was invited back here by Dustin." She matched his smile, turning to the reporters and their cameramen who were filming Dustin and Shayna right now.

"You have no business being here."

"You have no business messing with my life. I heard about the offer you made to Trent. I think you and I have a problem that you need to explain to me."

"We don't like your element in our sport and if helping out a damned hero of the rodeo accomplishes that goal, then we're damned glad to do it."

"Who's pulling your strings?" she asked.

"Is it that hard to believe that you're no longer wanted here?"

She wouldn't let him see how much that hurt her. "If you ever mess up a job opportunity for me again, I'm going to be your worst public relations nightmare. You think I'm a loose cannon now? Fuck with me again and see what happens. I'll show your audience the type of hero you have in Shayna James and her electric cattle prod."

"Stay away from Shayna and Dustin," he said.

"Make me," June replied, then sashayed away.

She went up to the happy couple as they were giving an interview. Coming up behind them on Dustin's side, she said to him, "Thanks."

When Dustin turned to her, June reached up and kissed him.

Shayna screeched. Camera phone flashes went crazy. And Dustin didn't push her away. The kiss did nothing for her and, in fact, she felt a little sick. She ended it before he got the bright idea of shoving his tongue into her mouth in front of his fiancée. As she sauntered out of the arena, she took a last look over her shoulder. Sinclair was holding Shayna back and Dustin was touching his lips as he watched her leave.

Seeing Sinclair and Shayna so close together, June wondered if her love child comment had been spot-on. They had the same blue eyes. Not just the color, but the shape. And there were other similarities, too—although she didn't think being an asshole was hereditary. She shook her head. That was just wishful thinking.

THEY MADE IT back in plenty of time for paint night. Emily was pissed that she missed all the drama. June felt like a weight had been lifted off her shoulders. Normally she would have celebrated with a glass of wine, but instead, she settled for the chilled pear nectar that Janice had set out for anyone who wanted it. It was a dry event and June was ridiculously touched.

Esteban came in with the rest of the guys from the ranch who had been roped into this event. April and Cole sat together on pillows that had been artfully arranged by a low easel. Kelly and Trent were seated in sturdy chairs with padded seats and a strong back. As the guests of honor, Emily and Donovan were at a table on a dais with an easel set up on it. Nate was nowhere to be seen, but Janice acted like the hostess and had a standing easel set up in the front of the room with her mother.

June wasn't used to a quiet night of fun with loving couples in normal relationships. A regular night for her was splitting a tab at a restaurant while everyone bickered and flirted, and you didn't know who you were going to go home with until last call.

Janice introduced their art instructor and as the man started his lesson, Esteban leaned into her. They were standing in the back.

"Tell me again why I let you talk me into this," he whispered in her ear.

It sent shivers up and down her spine.

"Barrel-racing lessons for your niece."

"Right." He squirted the paints into the plastic palette. "So I saw some interesting pictures on Instagram."

"Yeah, Emily and I went up to the stockyards."

"Did you compete?"

"No." She huffed out a laugh without any humor in it.

"Things looked like they got interesting."

"You could say that." She stared down at the brushes. Shayna and Sinclair, father and daughter? That *could* be the reason why Sinclair wanted June out of the way. Merry was good, but June was better. If June was still on the circuit, Shayna would have no chance of winning.

"I think I was set up," she whispered.

"What do you mean?" he said, cupping her cheek so she would look at him.

Quickly, she blinked away the tears that had been threatening. "I think I got pushed out. I think Shayna's got people making sure she gets the sixty thousand purse for the barrel-racing championship."

Esteban whistled softly through his teeth. "That's a lot of cash."

"It would have paid for Athena's care, hotels, gas and..." June looked down and wiggled her toes. "A new pair of boots."

"Who's behind it?"

"I think Shayna's father, but I'm not sure. I've got Emily doing some internet research."

"You need to put this in writing. Go straight to the top with your suspicions."

"I need proof first, but yeah, I should write a few emails and see where it gets me."

"Okay, class, that's how you begin," the instructor said. "Let's see your vision."

"I hope you were paying attention," June muttered.

"I got this." Esteban took a paintbrush and dipped it into the bluebonnet-blue paint.

The easel was a large one and June realized that she could stand to the side and fondle Esteban without anyone being able to see. The blue line he had been painting on the easel zig-zagged when she casually stroked her hand over his belt.

"You're going to tease me?" he said softly.

She slipped a key into his front pocket. "It's only teasing if I don't follow through."

"What's that?" he asked.

"I'm staying here tonight. Room three."

Esteban drew in a shaky breath. "How fast can we get through this?"

"I think an hour, maybe forty-five minutes."

"Then it's your turn to paint." Handing her the brush, he stood behind her.

She could feel his erection pressing into her backside. She swayed against him, loving the hard feel of him. As she tried to concentrate on the instructor's direction to recreate the sample painting he had up in the front, Esteban used the cover of the canvas on the easel to slip his hand up her shirt.

"I need to tell you that you're my fantasy woman," he whispered into her ear. "I've thought about you for years."

June bit back a gasp at the rough feel of his calloused palm on her belly. She painted blue circles as he found her hard nipple pressing against her bra. He rolled it gently between his thumb and forefinger and she ground her ass back into him. The instructor was making his way to the back of the room, so Esteban discreetly stopped caressing her. But he still held her close against him.

"That's an interesting take," the instructor said about their painting and moved along.

"We need to hurry things up," Esteban said in her ear.

"Why don't we take the paints up to the room," she suggested.

"Janice will kill me if we get paint on her sheets. However…" Esteban grabbed a large brush with a wide tip.

"What are you going to do with that?" she asked, intrigued.

"Wait and see." He stuck it in his back pocket.

The class finally wrapped up and June took her painting upstairs while Esteban said his goodbyes and pretended to leave. She wasn't sure why he was bothering. Janice knew what they were up to, and was without a doubt going to tell her sisters and probably her husband, too.

While she waited for Esteban to come upstairs, she got undressed. She was glad she'd seen Dustin today and felt nothing. It had been a long, lonely stay in her all-women's rehab center and her last memory of sex had been mixed with her anger at him. While the hurt was still there for his betrayal, it had lost the sharpness. She didn't want those memories forefront in her mind anymore. Given the way he'd acted this morning, it hadn't meant a damned thing to him. It had changed the course of her life, and yet he had gone on as if nothing out of the ordinary had happened.

Maybe it hadn't. June couldn't remember anything more than a few details. She wished she had a clearer picture of that night. From someone who was there that she trusted. Maybe she was crazy with the conspiracy theory that Sinclair was Shayna's father. But it made sense. The complaints about Shayna abusing her horse had never gone anywhere. Maybe Sinclair had intercepted them. It didn't seem fair that

June was blocked from competing when Shayna James had been right there in the mud with her. June might have blacked out from drinking too much, but Shayna had beat the hell out of her. So why wasn't Shayna out on her tight ass too…unless someone was covering it for her? Did Shayna deliberately go after Dustin, knowing June would go off on a bender? June couldn't shake the feeling that the whole fiasco had been planned.

But she didn't want to think about Shayna and Dustin anymore. It was bad enough that pictures of her and Dustin's kiss were all over the internet. She didn't want to be associated with him anymore. Right now, she wanted nothing more than to have the imprint of Esteban's body on hers so she could put Dustin's memory to rest, once and for all.

Naked, she lay on top of the covers facing the door. When Esteban walked in, he stumbled. Closing the door and locking it, he looked her up and down. She felt his gaze like a physical caress.

"You're beautiful enough to paint," he said, taking out the paintbrush.

Spreading her legs, she wondered what he had planned for that. He started with a gentle stroke down her nose and then tapped her on the chin lightly.

"I've thought about having you underneath me since the first time I saw you ride professionally. In your interview afterward, you were breathless and glowing. I think we were both eighteen or thereabouts."

The silky brush tickled as he trailed it over her jawline

and down her throat.

She wasn't sure why he wasn't already inside her. She liked foreplay as much as anyone, but right now, she wanted to be ridden hard and fast.

"Take off your clothes," June said.

"Come first." He swirled the brush around one of her nipples and then the other.

Her hips rose involuntarily, even as her nipples tightened more. Dipping his head down, he sucked one into his mouth. Tugging and licking, Esteban grazed his teeth over them, pulling on one and then letting it go with a loud pop.

"I should be kissing you first, but I couldn't resist." He trailed the paintbrush down to her belly and circled her belly button, dipping inside briefly before trailing down her legs, inside her thighs to her ankles and then through her toes. "You want to tell me about you and Dustin?"

"Not right now," she gasped. Every nerve ending she had was on fire. She wanted to clutch him to her, rip off his clothes, but she was riveted by the light caress and the anticipation of what he was going to do next.

"I'm going to have to insist." He went back to air brushing her nipples.

June forced back a groan. "We dated. It's over."

"It didn't look over."

"I did it to piss off Shayna. I'll tell you everything later. Fuck me. Now," she ordered, about to come out of her skin.

"I've jerked off to you for five years. We're doing this on my time."

"Please," she cajoled, biting her bottom lip.

"Did you come yet?" he asked, setting the paintbrush aside. Esteban dipped a finger between her thighs in a bold caress that had her spreading her legs wider. "You're wet." He fingered her lightly. "But not wet enough. I want you drenched."

Stretching down, he kissed her and used a second finger. His mouth was everything. Hot, sweet and demanding. Shivering, June unbuttoned his shirt. Esteban continued to slide his mouth over hers in the same leisurely way he had kissed her in his truck. But his fingers. Oh, his fingers were busy keeping her on the edge of pleasure. She liked the contrast of his silky mouth persuading her to open wider, while his fingers demanded a response.

She moaned as the friction built and gave herself up to him as she writhed on his hand and let him plunder her mouth. June could hear the wet sounds her body made as his fingers weaved over her folds to torment her clit.

Unable to take it, she flopped back on the bed while he strummed her like a guitar. His eyes were intense as he stared at her face.

"I'm coming," she whispered.

"Yes," he said. "You are."

It was like a sunburst inside her. She slammed her legs together and rode his fingers to a satisfying orgasm. While she recovered, he got undressed and joined her on the bed. Kissing him again, she entwined her legs through his and wrapped her arms around his back. The more his mouth pleasured hers, the more she wanted him. Her nipples felt hot against the muscles of his chest and his cock was velvety smooth and rock hard against her hip.

She had been expecting a quick hard fuck against the wall or bent over the couch. After all, he'd said she was his fantasy. June hadn't been expecting tenderness or him taking his time to explore her body.

It was sweet torture when his mouth left hers to graze his teeth against her throat. She moved to clutch his cock and stroke it while he licked and sucked every inch of her neck until he got down to her breasts.

He kissed slowly down her front to her belly and when he knelt between her thighs, June got self-conscious.

"You don't have to," she said. "I know some guys don't like…"

He stuck his tongue inside her and cupped her ass to his face.

June hung her thighs over his shoulder and gripped the sheets hard. "Oh," she said, her eyes locked on the ceiling as he licked her up and down. When he went for her clit, she lost her damn mind. She might have screamed as she came on his face. He held her there as she writhed and bucked and licked her to another orgasm that turned her inside out. What the actual hell? She never reacted to sex like this. Usually, it was a quick satisfying fuck and she was out and about. June wouldn't have been able to walk away now, if she'd wanted to. Her legs were a quivering useless wreck and every inch of her was an erogenous zone that begged for his touch.

"Damn, you taste amazing," he said resting his cheek on her thigh before kissing his way back up her front. The rasp of his beard on her belly, and the oversensitive peaks of her nipples, made her moan. He sucked on both of them before settling himself in between her thighs.

She closed her eyes in anticipation.

"I'll be right back."

"Don't you dare leave me like this," she swore.

Esteban rolled off the bed and trailed his fingers down her body.

Reaching out for him, she took his erection in her hand and slowly stroked him. "Just where do you think you're going?"

"Condom," he gasped out.

She nearly purred in satisfaction. "Not yet, you're not." Kneeling up on the bed, she stroked him, lifting her face up for more of his kisses. He cupped the back of her head and slid his tongue alongside hers.

It was his turn to moan as she rubbed him faster. She couldn't lie there passive anymore and let him pleasure her. She wanted him to come as well.

"I need to be inside you," he gritted out.

"Okay." June let him go to take the condoms out of his jeans, then took one from him and rolled it down over him. Pushing him back onto the bed, June straddled him and guided him inside her.

Her head rolled back as she sank onto him.

"Think you can stay on?" he asked.

"It had better be more than eight seconds."

"No promises," he gritted out as she leaned over to sway her breasts in his face while she bounced up and down on him.

"Yes," she cried out. This was what she wanted. What she needed. Hard, deep, fast. June felt like she was on a roller coaster, with the anticipation of the climb and the excitement as everything rushed to its conclusion.

Esteban's fingers dug into her ass as he thrust up into her. Clinging to his shoulders, she rode him fiercely as his mouth captured hers.

Leaning back, June held his head to her breasts as he surged forward. When he had her nipple back in his mouth, she sobbed in release as she came hard all over him. Gripping him tight, she floated on wave after wave of pleasure. She was boneless when he drove her from below, continuing to pound away.

She received him enthusiastically and he held her tight as he shuddered and emptied himself inside her.

Cheerfully, she wrapped her arms and legs around him. "That was worth waiting for," she said.

He smiled against her mouth. "Five years, probably more."

# Chapter Ten

I T HAD BEEN a hell of a day, a runaway calf, a broken fence, and the sun so hot, Esteban wanted to jump face first into the next water bucket he saw. He was hoping that June would join him tonight at the oasis for a little lovemaking under the stars, but she said she had something going on and would let him know. He wondered if she was blowing him off, if somehow, he had disappointed her last week. Esteban couldn't see how. They had made love four times, falling asleep in each other's arms before waking up and doing it again.

He had been damn useless the next day in the saddle, but for some reason, Nate had gone easy on him. He was pretty sure Janice had told Nate where Esteban had spent the night, and with whom, but Nate didn't mention it to him. Esteban made sure to work extra hard for the rest of the week.

The team had moved the herd to a new pasture today and because of that, they were going to work locally tomorrow, which put everyone in a good mood. It wasn't as exciting as riding out with the cows, but Esteban enjoyed maintaining the ranch area as a change of pace. He'd enjoy it a lot more when they hired more ranch hands.

Luis's first week was going well. He was fitting in quickly and learning the ropes without too much supervision. But Luis and their mother kept pressuring Esteban to get Sam on the payroll as well. She had already called him twice today. He hadn't bothered calling her back. Beatriz even texted that he needed to get Sam a job ASAP. They had moved her and Dina in last Saturday, without a problem. Cliff had had to spend the weekend in jail and didn't get out until Monday, which was glorious. He was also not happy to find his soon-to-be ex-wife packed and moved out with their daughter, but at least he was keeping things civil.

Esteban didn't bother trying to drum up conversation with Nate about the job on the ride back from the pasture. Nate would let him know when he had the green light from Emily. Sam and his family would just have to be patient.

"We're going to need to do some digging tomorrow for the new fences," Nate said when they reached the ranch.

Esteban nodded. He was dying to ask Nate what he knew about his fight with Cliff or his night with June, but he hadn't gotten to be assistant foreman by ticking off his boss. Nate would mention it, if he thought it was relevant.

As Esteban took his and Nate's horse back to the stable to put them away for the night, his stomach grumbled. He could smell the barbecue chicken that was tonight's dinner, and couldn't wait to dig in. Lunch had been six long hours ago.

Sarah Sullivan put out a good spread. She and her husband, Frank, came out every day and set up the chow wagon. Esteban swore her lemonade had a secret ingredient in it—

not too tart, not too sweet, and with a jolt of caffeine or something that was refreshing, even in the Texas summer.

All the ranch hands, however, took turns cooking dinner. Esteban's specialty was his abeula's pozole recipe. Only he used chopped steak instead of pork. His grandmother would have been appalled. He could almost hear her reprimand, "You don't mess with tradition." But what was the point in tradition, if you ignored ways to make things better?

After taking care of the horses, Esteban felt as if every inch of him was covered in sweat and trail dust. Wishing he had time to go for a swim at the oasis, he settled for a long shower. He didn't even care that Tony had used up most of the hot water.

The cool spray was just what he needed to feel human again. He was tired, though, and after he toweled off, he collapsed into his twin bed in the bunkhouse. As Nate's assistant, he warranted a private bedroom. He had never been so glad as when he'd been able to move out of the room he shared with Ringo. Ringo made a lot of noise in his sleep, from both ends.

Against his better judgment, he closed his eyes. It would be just his luck to sleep through dinner. Maybe Luis would save him a plate. Yeah, like that would ever happen. His phone rang. He hoped it was June. But it was Sam.

"Yeah," he said.

"Anything?" He sounded as eager as a black Lab puppy.

Groaning, Esteban hoisted himself to his feet. He had better get dressed for dinner. "No. Don't you think I would have told you?"

"Should I come by and talk to Nate myself?"

"No, that'll only piss him off. Look, he said we're probably going to hire someone soon. You're the only one he's considering. Just play it cool and chill." Tucking the phone into his shoulder, Esteban dropped the towel around his waist and rooted through his drawers for some clean clothes to wear to dinner.

"I need the job, bro."

"I know." Esteban rubbed a hand over his face.

"No, you don't know. Anne's pregnant."

Esteban fumbled the phone and almost dropped it. "What?"

His brother kept talking. "Her parents kicked her out when she told them."

"Oh no," he said.

"It gets worse."

"Is she all right? Are Beatriz and Dina all right?" Esteban's mind raced with all the possibilities.

"Chill," Sam said. "Everyone's fine. Mamá said she could stay here. Only she and Beatriz would have to share a room."

"That's a definite test of your relationship."

"I need to get out of here, man. We're looking for apartments, but without me having a steady job, no one will rent to us."

"I'm doing my best here," Esteban said, pulling on his underwear.

"I've got a line on a short-term job in Dallas. It's only for a few weeks. I can't afford to pass it up."

"I understand," Esteban said, stepping into his favorite

pair of jeans—soft and faded from countless wearing and washings.

Sam had been filling in as a ranch hand on a ton of farms all across Texas, but it was piecemeal work. A month here. A week there. Lately, the jobs had been few and far between.

"I can start at the Three Sisters Ranch the very next day after the contract ends. I don't care if I have to drive all night to get back there. Do you think it will ruin my chances if I take the Dallas job?"

"No," Esteban said quickly. "Take it."

"Can you let Nate know that I can start tomorrow, just in case?"

"Take the job in Dallas." Esteban pulled a black T-shirt over his head and started tucking it into his pants. "If he's ready to hire someone before the contract is up, I'm sure I can convince him to wait for you. We've been shorthanded for almost a year now. What's a few more days?"

A few more back-breaking days.

"Are you sure?" Sam asked.

"Don't worry. I'll see what I can do."

"I'm counting on you."

Like he needed any more pressure on him about this. Esteban pushed that thought back down into the far reaches of his brain. He loved his family, but they tended to think he was a miracle worker. Maybe it was because he made it a point to do the impossible whenever he could.

"I'll let you know as soon as I hear anything," Esteban said, sitting down to put on his socks and boots.

"All right. Love you, bro."

"Love you too, kid."

Jeez, just when he was ready to get annoyed with Sam, his brother said something like that.

JUNE WAS STARTING to think she had an unhealthy obsession with Shayna James. She wrote several emails to Shelby Miller, the CEO of the Women's Professional Rodeo Circuit. One was a complaint about Sinclair. Another was a complaint about Shayna's treatment of her horse. And yet another respectfully asking to be allowed back to compete.

It left a bad taste in her month. It reeked of desperation, and she hated it.

Emily had found nothing connecting Shayna's mother to Sinclair Thompson.

"They look alike," June said, leaning over Emily's laptop. She brought up a picture of Sinclair and Shayna. "See. Look at their chins."

"You're buggin'," Emily said, and added June's picture. "You're seeing what you want to. Look, you all have the same nose." Emily cackled when June shoved her.

"I can't just stay here and do nothing."

"What are you going to do?"

"I'm not sure. But I can't do anything from here." June ran a hand through her hair. "I'm going to see if I can find anyone who remembers what happened that night. I need to know."

"Just be careful," Emily said, with a concerned frown.

After draining her bank account, June put in a tank of gas. Then she pulled up Shayna's schedule. She was in Texas all this week. June didn't care if she had to sleep in her truck and eat instant noodles and peanut butter and jelly sandwiches—she was going to get to the bottom of this.

She'd let her mother think she was helping Merry, but she told Emily the truth. Emily was worried June was going to go to jail this time, but June never went near Shayna. She stuck to the crowd or the stands, but she drove all over Texas, spending most of the time observing Shayna and the way she treated people. Shayna didn't like riding. It was obvious.

Why would you ride on the rodeo circuit if you didn't love it? Why would you compete unless you couldn't wait to get back in the saddle? It didn't make any sense. But the longer she watched, she saw what Shayna wanted. Shayna did a lot more promotional work than Merry or June had ever done. Shayna was a commodity, which explained the way she rode. She wasn't in it for the race or for the competition. Shayna was a model, an actress and a spokesperson. She was the face of the WPRC. And June had cut off her ponytail.

Broke, disgusted and unsure of what to do with this information, June dejectedly headed back to her truck. With a championship to her name, Shayna could get a lot more modeling jobs. When she got into the parking lot, she saw someone taking a nap on the hood of her truck. "What the hell?"

It wasn't until she ran up that she recognized the dusty

cowboy boots and the hat over her face.

"Get off my truck, you heifer or I'll rope and tie you."

"I'd like to see you try," Merry said, raising the hat off her face.

"What are you doing here?" June asked, crossing her arms. "You're supposed to compete in Amarillo tonight."

"I've got a friend with a private plane."

"Must be nice." June made a face. She used to have friends like that. Now, no one called or returned her texts.

"It is nice." Merry hoisted herself up and jumped down. "But I think the better question is, what the fuck are you doing here?"

"There better not be an ass-shaped dent in my hood," June groused.

"Answer me," Merry said.

"It's not like I've got anywhere else to be," she said, flapping her arms to her sides.

Merry's face softened into something like pity and June's temper spiked.

"You can help me, if you want," Merry said.

"No, I don't want." That was all she needed, to see that pity on everyone else's face.

"You've got to stop stalking Shayna. She's too stupid to notice, but other people have. That's why I'm here."

"Why are you warning me off?" June asked.

"That little stunt you pulled with Dustin has put that bitch on the warpath. She's got a lot of friends who would like to drag you out behind the barn and make an example of you." Merry held up a hand when June would have spoken.

"She's got to go through me first. But I'm using up favors, trying to keep you safe at events like this."

"This is bullshit," June said. "She can't do this."

"She can as long as she's got a chance at winning. As soon as I beat her and she's number two, her popularity will fade."

"I'm not sure about that. She's their brand, their face."

"Second place is first loser, and no one wants a loser as their brand."

"The camera loves her," June said.

"No one else does."

Seeing how determined Merry was about making sure Shayna James was going to pay for what she did to her, June felt at a loss. Where did that leave her? There was still Sinclair.

June touched her forehead to Merry's. "I'm sorry I can't be the one to take her down. What do you need from me?"

"Stay home. Don't distract me. I'll see you at Emily's wedding."

"No." June pushed aside her pride. "I will come help you out. I'm afraid of what Shayna or Sinclair will do to you…or to Raphael. I don't put anything past them."

"If anyone touches my horse, it will be the last thing they ever do."

"Let me grab Athena and I'll meet you at your next event."

"The hell you will." Merry gripped her shoulders. "Shayna has put a bounty on you."

"A what?" June scoffed in disbelief.

"She wants to shave you bald."

June gasped. "That's perfect. I can be bait, and we can catch her in the act. Then maybe, I can leverage that to get back on the circuit."

"No," Merry said. "That's not what we're about. We ride horses and we compete with good sportsmanship. I don't give a flying fuck about followers or likes or whatever the new thing is."

"Tell that to Sinclair and Shayna," June grumbled.

"I don't have to."

"Well, maybe I do," June said stubbornly.

"Her value to the company, to Sinclair, to herself, is based on her winning. She's not going to beat me."

"Just…" June sighed. "Just don't drink anything you haven't had with you the whole time, okay?"

Merry narrowed her eyes. "What aren't you telling me?"

"Nothing." June looked into her sister's furious eyes. "I just know that I don't get blackout drunk."

"You drank a lot that night," Merry said ruefully.

"Still…" June rubbed the back of her neck. "Can you ask around and see if anyone we trust saw what actually happened?"

Merry kicked her tire in aggravation. "Don't you think I've already done that? Don't you think I would have told you?"

"What did you find out?"

"Nobody saw anything." Merry flung her hands up. "I can't pick my teeth without someone sharing that all over the internet. One of the juiciest fights in rodeo? Not a single picture. Not a single upload."

"Because it was a setup. That's my proof," June said excitedly. "The lack of proof is the proof."

"Yeah, well good luck making that work for you," Merry said.

"Someone saw something. I can dig out the truth."

"Bald." Merry pulled her hair and made scissors with her fingers.

"It's worth it." June paced back and forth in front of her truck. "You've got to talk to Dustin. He was acting weird, as if he didn't know that I'd been in rehab."

"You want me to talk to that two-timing snake?" Merry sneered.

June stopped in her tracks. "You mean, you didn't?"

"He's been avoiding me." Merry looked away. "It might be because I threatened to kick him so hard, he could wear his ass like a hat."

"Please, if you want me to go back home, you have to promise me that you'll talk to him."

"Fine." Merry rolled her eyes. "I'm not kissing him, though. Not even to piss off Shayna."

"Be careful," June said. "I should really come with you."

"No. I've got this. I've got plenty of friends who'll watch my back."

"So you don't need me?" June sniffed. She was not going to cry. Not here. Not now.

"I will always need my sister," Merry said. "But you need to have a life outside of the WPRC right now. You deserve to be happy. You're carrying around a lot of anger and it's consuming you."

"You sound like Linda," June groaned. "What the hell do I do with myself?"

"Call Emily. She's got an idea," Merry said. "I've got to get going. Stay out of trouble."

June held on tight to her sister, practically biting her tongue to beg her to stay. Merry would, but it would kill her standings and hurt her long game against Shayna. That was the difference between them. June was for the short payoff; Merry was content to wait for it.

June drove her back to the airstrip and watched Merry get into her friend's plane. She could hear the party music coming from it all the way in her truck and wondered if she'd made a mistake by not going with her. June missed the rodeo life.

She couldn't shake the thought that the best had already happened and she had to face this nothingness for the next sixty years. Who was she without the rodeo?

As she drove the long ride back to Last Stand, she wanted to call Esteban and talk with him. She wanted to hear his voice, but she didn't want to explain where she had been all this week.

So she called Emily instead and put the call through Bluetooth so she could safely talk while she drove.

"You ratted me out to Merry."

"Yes, I did," Emily admitted without a grain of shame.

"I was working on a plan," June said, feeling defensive. "I was going to see if I could take some pictures of Shayna abusing her horse, but I couldn't get close enough."

"Merry had a plan. You were just getting in the way."

"Well, what else am I supposed to do? I'm sick of just sitting around waiting for summer to be over so maybe I can start working at Trent's." June had spoken to April about starting her own business at another location, but the numbers made her head spin. Long story short, June couldn't afford the start-up.

"You could always come work for me," she said.

"And do what?"

"Well," Emily said. "Last year we had to lay off a bunch of ranch hands because we couldn't afford them. I've recently came into some money through an investor in the ranch, so we're trying to build back up to where we were before all the money problems got out of control."

"Ranch hand, huh." June considered it. She knew what was required. Working outside and with animals appealed to her better than any of the alternatives. She'd have longer days than she was used to, but it beat the hell out of being tied to a desk all day. "You're not just offering me a job because you feel sorry for me?" Because June wasn't about to take charity. She didn't want Emily to think she was looking for a handout. She'd get by. She always did.

"I'm your friend." Emily sighed. "I am sorry that you've made a colossal fuck-up of your life, that's for damned sure. But I really do need another ranch hand and you really need a job. What's the point in being the boss, if you can't do something nice for your friends?"

Well, when she put it like that…

"Would I be working with Esteban?"

"Duh, yeah. He'd be your supervisor."

"I'm sleeping with him. I meant we slept together. Well, we napped together and had lots of sex."

"Shut the front door. Why didn't you tell me this?" Emily squealed.

June squirmed. "I figured Janice did."

"You told Janice before me?" Emily sounded outraged.

"Well, I needed the room in her retreat center after paint night. I guess this means the whole ranch doesn't know?"

"No one's said a word to me."

"Maybe I should run it by Esteban first," June said.

"You're going to ask him for permission?"

"No, of course not. I just don't want to put him in an awkward position."

"Are you two dating?"

"Well, no."

"So it was a one-night stand?"

"I kind of wanted another night or two."

"But it's nothing serious?"

"Of course not," June scoffed, but a part of her was wondering who she was trying to convince.

"Then it's no big deal. You'll get to work together."

"I would like to see more of him." June thought it would be nice to spend the days with him. She liked how he made her feel when they were together.

"There you go."

Maybe this would be a good transition from the rodeo to real life. It couldn't hurt. It would pay some bills and keep her occupied until the season was over or until she heard back from the CEO of WPRC. "When can I start?" June asked.

"As soon as possible. If you can begin before my wedding, I can go on my honeymoon and not have to worry about your dumb ass. The pay's not much, but it includes room and board. You're welcome to stay in the bunkhouse, but you'd be the only woman."

A few lewd and lascivious images rolled through her brain of sneaking into Esteban's bed at night, but that was a recipe for disaster. So was living in a house full of male roommates. Reality won over the fantasy. She couldn't deal with living with just one man—she'd hate living with a bunch of them.

"No thanks," June said. "If I can't make the drive from Mama's, I'll sleep in my truck."

"You can also stay in one of Janice's retreat rooms, if she's not using it."

That sounded good and if Esteban wanted to visit her in room number three, that would be even better. "That would save me an hour or so in the morning. I'm assuming Nate wants us all there by dawn?"

"Try four a.m."

June winced.

"Earlier, if you want breakfast."

Maybe she'd rethink the bunkhouse. As long as her door had a lock, it would be like living in a college dorm room. Unfortunately, this would probably be the death knell of her and Esteban's budding romance. She had no business even thinking about getting involved with someone again, and yet, Esteban made her want to change all her rules about dating.

"What kind of jobs would I be doing?" June asked. She worked on enough farms in between rodeos to know she wasn't going to be sitting idle.

"We're concentrating on irrigation at the moment. You'll be doing maintenance on ditches, pipes, and other repairs. Are you still good at fixing tractors?"

"I'm a little rusty, but I know my way around an engine." Merry's father, Luke, had been a mechanic and he'd thought it was a good idea to teach her and her sisters how to change their own tires and do routine maintenance on their cars. When Mama had to work, he'd let them hang out in the garage as long as they were quiet. April read. Merry watched the television in the lounge. June had pulled up a stool and watched the mechanics work, picking up a few things while handing them tools. Mostly how to curse, but also what went wrong with the big farm equipment. "Do you have something you want me to look at?"

"Probably. Nate will assign you the job. Sun up, sun down, seven days a week, but not in a row. You'll be put on the rotation. Expect to work weekends for a while. But anyone who works Saturdays and Sundays get two days off in a row in the middle of the week. Of course, you'll have my wedding weekend off."

June smiled and felt hope for the first time since Trent had dropped the news on her. This job wasn't forever, but it would be good to keep her busy and best of all, she'd be on a horse for most of the day. Emily had really come through for her and June blinked fast to keep tears at bay. "I'm not afraid of hard work," she said.

"Good. Because Nate's not going to go easy on you just because you're my friend."

"I wouldn't want him to."

"There's just one thing," Emily said.

*Uh-oh.*

"There's a lot of drinking that goes on after work. I don't want to put you in a bad situation."

Oh, was that all? For a moment, June had thought Emily was going to tell her to tone down her attitude. That would've been impossible. She could play well with others, but she didn't have the time or patience to keep her mouth shut if she saw something she didn't like.

"I handled your bachelorette party okay, didn't I?"

"I don't remember."

"I've got pictures, but I'm saving them for the wedding reception. We're going to rent a screen and a projector. My favorite was of you and the strippers, doing shots off...well never mind, I don't want to spoil the surprise."

"That never happened," Emily said hotly. And then a few seconds later. "Did it? Of course, it didn't. You're an asshole." Emily snickered. "You'll fit right in with the ranch hands."

"I hope to," June said. It would be nice to finally have a place where she belonged and was accepted. She was pretty sure Sinclair Thompson couldn't touch her out on the range.

# Chapter Eleven

AGAINST HIS BETTER judgment, Esteban slapped on some cologne. He'd probably get razzed something fierce by the guys, but it reminded him of June. He had been going nonstop with family drama, hard long days at work, and falling exhausted into bed every evening. He barely had time to text her, but he had their date at Emily's wedding to look forward to. She hadn't been around either, according to the quick flashes he got from her Snapchat.

He was glad he put in the effort because when he went outside for dinner, Emily and June were there. Emily had brought over a large salad for everyone to share and also a smaller container of tofu or something not meat for herself. June had her arms full, passing out the bread baskets that Emily's mother had sent over.

She hadn't seen him yet. He wasn't sure how to play this. He wanted to sweep her in his arms and kiss her, but he didn't want to embarrass her. While he considered what to do, Frenchie and Ringo hurried over to help June. Esteban might have body-checked Tony in his rush to sit across from her when she stretched to grab a plate from Luis.

"Hey there," she said.

"This is a nice surprise," he said.

"Just wait." Her eyes sparkled with mischief.

"You got a fast horse," Luis said, joining them at the table.

Nate grunted from the head of the table. "I'm surprised Emily gave her back to you."

June helped herself to a roll and slathered butter on it. "I'm just fortunate she was able to give Athena the exercise that she needed while I was gone."

"Where have you been?" Ringo asked.

"Oh, here and there," she said, evading getting into it.

"I've seen every rodeo you've been in," Tony said.

"Wow, every one? Thank you." June smiled and Esteban could tell it was genuine. She didn't seem to get annoyed or tired of her fans. He liked that about her.

Esteban wanted her attention, but couldn't get a word in edgewise, even if he knew what to say. He wanted to stand out from the group. Maybe he'd take a page from Nate's book and be the strong, silent type.

Emily stood up while they were eating. She liked to give speeches. Luckily, she didn't care if they didn't stop what they were doing.

"Everybody, this is June Grayson."

"I think they know that," Nate grumbled.

"June, this is Nate. He's the foreman."

"Janice told me all about you. Just the good parts," June said.

Emily smacked her lightly. "Don't lie."

"Yeah, I don't have any good parts," Nate said, taking a

deep pull of his beer.

"This is Esteban, he's Nate's right-hand man."

Esteban gave Emily a sharp look. What on earth was she doing? She'd seen them together at paint night. Even if June hadn't told her they had been intimate, Emily didn't need to introduce June to him and Nate as if they were strangers.

He decided to play along just in case he missed something. "It's a pleasure to meet you, ma'am." Reaching across the table, he shook June's hand. She blushed, and he wished they were alone.

"I'm Luis, his brother. I'm a big fan. I always wanted to meet you," Luis said.

Now that Esteban thought of it, only Trent knew he had more than a passing interest in June. Even Luis didn't know the extent of their budding romance. Esteban had assumed that the gossip would be all over the ranch by now, but realistically they hadn't spent much time together. Even though the time they had spent together had been intense.

"It's nice to meet you, Luis," she said.

Emily went down the line introducing the four other ranch hands. Tony, Ringo, Frenchie, and Bob put on their best manners, and their knives and forks down to shake her hand. Frenchie even kissed the back of her hand, which made Esteban want to punch him in his smarmy face when June blushed a bit for him too.

"Don't mind him. He thinks he's Casanova," Ringo said.

"Casanova was Italian. I'm from Paris."

"Paris, Texas," Bob snorted.

Esteban wasn't sure how full of shit Frenchie was about

his background. He put on a good accent that got a little deeper when he was around pretty women. But he was a hard worker and a good friend, and at the end of the day, that was all Esteban cared about.

"Can I get you a beer?" Frenchie asked her.

June's smile froze on her face.

"No, thank you," Emily said.

June arched her a look and also answered. "I'll take a seltzer, if you're getting up."

Her voice was a low, sexy drawl that raised the hair on his forearms.

How the hell was he going to stake his claim on her with this crowd? He should have kissed her in front of everyone. Right now, he had to get his lady her drink.

"I got it." He waved Frenchie to sit. Untangling himself from the picnic table, he went over to the cooler, taking out a beer for himself and a lemon seltzer for June.

"Cheers," she said, clinking the can against his.

"So where have you been these last couple of months?" Frenchie asked, circling back. "You missed a few events."

"Yeah." June looked down at her plate. "About that."

Esteban felt a little protective of her. It wasn't anyone's business, but before he could say anything, Emily jolted to her feet.

"I have some great news," she blurted out. "I know things have been real tight lately and I wanted to thank each and every one of you for sticking it out and helping us keep the ranch afloat."

*Where was this going?* Esteban thought, shooting a glance

at Nate.

But Nate was frowning at Emily, while the rest of the ranch hands were acknowledging her thanks with nods and toasting her with their beers.

"We've hired another new ranch hand today."

*Wait. What?*

Nate upped his frown to a full-on glower.

"June is going to be working here from now on with you as one of the ranch hands."

It was all Esteban could do not to storm away, but there wasn't a dignified way to maneuver out of a picnic table. Nate's back tensed up, but he concentrated on his plate instead of continuing to glare at Emily, who was his boss after all. The guys whooped and cheered and started pestering June with questions.

"What about the rodeo?"

"Don't you have a championship to take back from your sister?"

"Is there something wrong with your horse?"

"Are you going to stay in the bunkhouse with us?"

"You can share my room," Ringo said.

*The hell she could.*

Nate slapped his hand on the table, and everyone shut up. "That's enough. I'm more interested to know if you've done this sort of thing before, Miss Grayson."

"Call me June. And yes, I have."

Esteban swallowed down his anger and deliberately drained his beer in one long swallow. He forced himself to set it back on the table, so that she wouldn't see that he'd rather throw it across the ranch. Why didn't she tell him? It should have been Sam sitting there. Sam. God. Sam. How was he going to let him know? Actually, Luis was furiously texting under the table.

Well, that was one thing he could cross off his list. His entire family was finding out at the same time he was. He shut off his phone.

"You want to elaborate on that?" Nate said. "I apologize for interviewing you after the fact, but it's not like I had a chance to do it before you were hired."

"Nate," Emily snapped.

Some of the tension left Esteban's spine. At least Nate hadn't known about it, either. Otherwise, he would have given Esteban a heads-up. Still, his mother was going to lose her shit, and Esteban was never going to hear the end of it from his family. After all, he all but promised Sam the job and now June had taken it. This was going to delete all the goodwill he was trying to build up for her with his mother when she'd agreed to train Dina.

June held up a hand to stop Emily, who had taken in a deep breath to lay into Nate. "He's got a point, Emily. You probably should have told him first." Tucking her hair back behind her ear, June leaned forward and addressed Nate. "I'm sorry for the shock, but I'm qualified. I've dug holes for fence posts, driven tractors and fixed them. I've been around horses all my life and can help with any injuries they get. I don't have a lot of experience with cattle, but I was on the pro rodeo circuit for the past fourteen years. While my primary success was with barrel racing, I've won several first-place prizes in roping events."

"Heeler or breakaway?" Nate asked.

"Both. I've won circuit titles in breakaway and tie-down roping. The team roping, I did with my sister, Merry. We took turns being the header and the heeler."

"That's two different types of throws," Nate said.

"Yeah, thanks for mansplaining that," June said.

Emily cleared her throat. Esteban held in a snort of laughter with effort. Laughter? Hell, he needed to get a grip and remember he was pissed at her.

"What? My sister and I are title holders in that event, too. I've roped steer in under ten seconds, throwing as both a header and as a heeler. We both have."

"All right," Nate drawled.

June's whole being lit up when she talked about rodeo and watching her face come alive with joy made Esteban forget about his anger for a bit. If she hadn't stolen his brother's job, he probably would have liked working with her.

"When are you starting?"

"Monday," Emily said.

Nate grunted. "Be here by four a.m."

"Okay," June said.

After an awkward moment of silence, dinner resumed but the conversation was stilted. June and Emily finished up quickly and got up to leave.

"See you boys on Monday," June said, not meeting his gaze.

Their goodbyes weren't as enthusiastic as their hellos

were, and Esteban again felt a twinge. Still, he couldn't keep his gaze from lingering on June as she and Emily got back into the ATV and rode back to the main house.

Why hadn't she given him a heads-up? Last he knew, she was going to be an instructor at Trent's school. But she hadn't said anything. Granted, they hadn't exchanged more than a few words since paint night, but she could have tried.

He wanted to text her, *WTF?*, but considering the way his brother's phone was blowing up, Esteban decided that he would wait.

"That ain't fair," Tony said.

"Life's not fair," Nate said. "Get used to it."

"Do we have to be on our best behavior now?" Ringo said, gathering up the dirty plates to take into the kitchen to be washed.

"Why start now?" Nate said, getting up from the table.

Esteban followed him to the large trash container.

"It should have been Sam." He said it quietly, so only Nate could hear.

"I know," Nate said. "I don't want to string him along, but that rodeo queen isn't going to last a month. She's too high-maintenance. You can tell just by looking at her."

"How do you know?" Esteban asked, intrigued in spite of himself.

"The pretty ones always are. And I will not stand for any bullshit."

"So you want us to give her a hard time, boss?" Frenchie asked, dumping his trash out as well.

"Shit no. Don't be an asshole. And if I hear that you are

being a dick, it's my boot up your ass. Got it?"

Frenchie held up his hands in surrender and since it was his turn to do the dishes, he carried some back in the house.

"She'll be out of here as soon as the WPRC crooks their little finger. And when that happens, we'll get your brother to replace her. I'll guarantee that."

"I appreciate it," Esteban said. But the thought of June leaving didn't make him feel any better.

Nate was right, though. Women like June didn't work in places like this. She was used to being in the spotlight and air-conditioning. She'd get sick of being a ranch hand, real quick. In fact, he'd give her two weeks, tops. By that time, Sam would be done with his gig in Dallas. Emily would find another job for her, so she wouldn't have to go too far. And they could continue with what they started. The rest of the tension left his body. It was all going to work out.

"I hate to ask it, but if it comes to her wanting to stay in the bunkhouse, do you mind giving up your room?" Nate asked.

Esteban did mind—it wasn't as if she could double up with one of the men. "Yeah, I'll start getting my things together. Is there any way I don't have be in the same room as Ringo?"

"I don't care. Pick your roommate."

June would be his first choice, even if he was mad that she weaseled his brother out of a job, but he wasn't about to say that aloud. "I'll take Frenchie." That way, he could keep an eye on him.

"Works for me." Nate got up from the table. "We still

have plenty of spots to fill. We need to hire more hands. We got room for four more. We'll get Sam in here, one way or the other."

"Thanks," Nate said. Now, all he had to do was get June alone so he could find out what the hell had happened.

# Chapter Twelve

JUNE HAD BARELY slept the night before, so she was more or less awake when her alarm went off at two thirty in the morning. She had dodged Esteban's calls ever since Emily hired her. She should have given him a heads-up and allowed him to react however he wanted. If it cost her the job, she should have sucked it up. What she did was unfair and she owed him an apology.

Two thirty in the morning was when she usually went to bed. The night air always made her feel shaky cold, but that could have been the nerves. June parked in the bunkhouse parking lot an hour later and then stood outside of her truck, looking around. She didn't hear anyone moving inside the bunkhouse, and the lights were off. Rubbing her arms, she wondered if she dared go back into the truck for a quick snooze. But just as she thought about it, a light came on inside.

She still didn't feel comfortable about going in, so she sat outside on the picnic bench and obsessed over Shayna James's Instagram. Damn, she missed the circuit. She missed the people, the horses, and yeah, the parties. But she didn't miss Shayna. Not a damned bit.

June's life had been way too quiet lately and there was a gnawing fear at the back of her throat that this was her new normal.

Unaccustomed panic set in and she scrambled to her feet. June headed for the bunkhouse when she started to smell bacon cooking. The door wasn't locked, so she let herself in. There was a large common room area that smelled vaguely of beer and feet. A large couch and a couple of recliners faced a widescreen television that was currently off. She heard pots and pans rattling in what had to be the kitchen.

She walked in and was surprised to see Esteban there. In front of him, there was an enormous cast-iron frying pan that he was pouring eggs into.

"Hey," she said.

"Hey," he said, putting the bowl in the sink. "You're early."

"Nate said four." She scowled.

"Four is when we need to be down here, dressed for breakfast. I guess he wanted to give you some wiggle room."

"Or he expected me to be late, because I'm a woman." June crossed her arms over her chest.

"I don't know about that," Esteban said diplomatically.

She sighed and rubbed her hands together to get some warmth in them. "I owe you an apology."

He didn't say anything. Great, he wasn't going to make this any easier on her.

"Do you need help? I can make the coffee," she said.

"That's the first thing I did." He pointed to the barrel-size urn that was plugged into the wall.

"Is it ready?"

"Give it a few. We take turns with breakfast and dinner. Now that you're here, we can each take a day. Have you got a specialty?"

June smirked. "I burn water."

Esteban winced. "Well, I guess we'll force it down. You're going to want to eat as much as you can—at least for breakfast and lunch. The Sullivan family provides that. You're going to need the fuel."

She wasn't a big breakfast eater.

"You can grab the two loaves of bread and start putting them on the cookie sheet for toast."

"Toast in the oven?"

"Same with the bacon. It's quicker to do a lot that way." He pulled two trays of bacon out and set them on the counter. As she placed the slices of bread on the cookie sheet, she watched as he picked the bacon up out of the grease with tongs and placed the strips on a stainless-steel rack.

"That's smart," she said.

"I guess there's not a lot of time to do your own cooking on the road?"

"Not too much. If I bothered with breakfast, it was take-out. Merry and I would occasionally set up a slow cooker in our rooms for dinners. Easy chili or stew. It was nice to come home to a hot meal that wasn't deep-fried."

With the breakfast prep done, Esteban poured them both a mug of coffee and placed them on the small kitchen table. "Have a seat. What happened to teaching barrel racing at Trent's place?"

"Right," she said, launching into the details about Sinclair Thompson's deal that Trent couldn't refuse.

Esteban's demeanor thawed and he became angry on her behalf. "That's bullshit."

"It is," she said. "But don't worry. Your niece will still get her free lessons, just not from me. How are things going with that?"

"My sister Beatriz and Dina moved in with my mom. It's tough, especially with all the people in the house."

She reached across the small table and laid a hand on his. "When Emily offered me this job, I grabbed it. But I shouldn't have let you be blindsided by the announcement."

"Why did you?"

June shook her head. "I'm not sure. A part of me thought you wouldn't care, and it would be a nice surprise. And another part of me thought you wouldn't want me here, and I didn't want to hear that."

"I don't want you here," he said.

"Ouch," she said, surprised at how much the truth hurt.

Esteban opened his mouth to say more, but his brother came in. Luis did a double take, then scowled at her. After he got his cup of coffee, he stormed out.

"What was that all about?" she asked.

"Well," Esteban started to say, but then, one by one, the rest of the ranch hands trickled into the kitchen and then outside to the larger picnic table area.

"Grab a plate and sit down out there. We can talk more after work."

"Right," she said. She was too nervous to eat, so she just

refilled her coffee.

The men had a routine about the start of their day, and she felt in the way. There was a lot of testosterone out there in the small area and she escaped into the common area with her coffee the first chance she got. She wasn't sure if everyone was just a grumpy bastard in the morning or if it was because she was there.

*It's better than moping around Mama's trailer*, she thought.

As the ranch hands filed past her with their brimming plates, she figured it was safe to go back into the kitchen. Esteban was cleaning up the pans in between bites of food. Even though she didn't want it, she made herself a bacon and egg sandwich and sat at the small table.

"Plate and silverware go in the dishwasher when you're done and then we set it to run. Whoever's turn it is to do dinner…"

"Tony," June said, looking at the schedule. She saw that she was doing breakfast on Saturday and dinner on Sunday.

"It'll be his job to unload the breakfast dishes and load the supper ones back up."

"What's for dinner?" she asked.

"Ziti and meatballs," he said.

"Do you think it's okay if I make lasagna for Saturday night?" she said.

"I thought you couldn't cook."

"I can't, but my Mama can. It's her specialty."

Esteban snorted. "How many marriage proposals you want?"

She snorted back. "None, but I'll pass them on to Mama. She's due for another marriage soon."

Did that sound bitter? June didn't mean it to come out that way. She just didn't understand why her mother put herself through all that. The only thing marriage ever got her mother was paperwork and heartache. It didn't keep her husbands home or faithful. If anything, the moment they were married, they stopped being fun.

"Marriage isn't so bad."

"So I keep hearing," June said. "But you still have to convince me."

"I'd like to, if you give me a chance."

June's eyes widened and her heartbeat picked up. The thought of it was crazy and yet, it gave her a thrill that she hadn't felt since she was in the rodeo. "Aren't you my supervisor now?" she asked, trying for a joke. It was getting too serious in here all of a sudden.

"I won't tell HR, if you won't."

"Considering Emily is HR, she pretty much already knows. I'd be open to some convincing. Just don't get your hopes up," she said.

"I bet I can convince you to settle down."

"Settling down has always equaled boring to me," she said. "But I might not have a choice."

Esteban frowned. "Are you pregnant?"

This time she laughed. "No, there's not a chance of that."

"That a fact?" he said.

"Absolutely. I'm on the pill and you used a condom."

She wondered how much time they had until Nate got there or one of the other ranch hands barged back into the kitchen. A good-morning kiss would soothe out some of the ragged edges she was feeling.

"What are you looking at?" he drawled.

"You."

"Like what you see?"

"You know I do." She darted her tongue over her lips.

He looked away.

"Something wrong?" she asked.

"We need to talk, but it's got to be somewhere private where we're not going to be interrupted."

"Sugar, if you find a place like that, talking is the last thing that's going to be on my mind."

He closed his eyes and his hands clutched the counter. At least, he still felt the same crazy attraction that she did. She didn't need a man to be happy. But she wanted one. This one.

June slowly uncoiled from her seat. Stretching, she watched his eyes drop to her waist. But unlike her usual attire, she had tucked her shirt in and was wearing a bra that was sturdy instead of pretty.

At that moment, Nate walked in. "If you ladies are done here in the kitchen," he said. "I'm going to need you outside so we can get this day started."

Flustered, Esteban grabbed his plate and hers and put them in the dishwasher.

"I'm not going to have a problem with you, am I?" Nate asked her in a tone that set her teeth on edge.

"Why should you be any different?" June bumped her hip into Nate as she passed by.

Nate grunted in disgust.

June headed out to the ranch hands' stable where she had left Athena last night. Athena whickered to her as June led her out into the corral so she could saddle up. She planned to ride her only a few days a week, and then take one of the Sullivan horses the rest of the time. While Athena needed the exercise, June didn't want to risk her getting hurt.

After everyone was in the saddle, Nate briefed them on what he wanted them to do. He paired her up with Esteban and sent them out to dig some fence poles and do repair work. It was going to be hot, dusty work. She was definitely going to earn her pay today.

"Supposed to be ninety round noon," she said to Esteban once they picked up a few extra gallons of water.

"Could be worse," he said.

June waited for him to mention what was up or make a comment about them being all alone with no one around for miles to see. But he didn't say a word. June wasn't used to the silence and after a few moments, she became uncomfortable.

"We're alone. Let's talk."

He shook his head. "No, this is business. We keep the personal stuff out of it until after hours."

"You're the boss," she said.

But the silence was killing her. To fill the void, she started talking about obvious things. "I'm glad we'll have the bulk of the work done before lunchtime, when the heat gets really bad."

"We're going to finish before lunch. It's a half hour ride to where the chuck wagon is. You brought gloves, right?"

She hadn't. "You could have mentioned that before we left."

"I thought you'd done this before."

Gritting her teeth, she bit down a snarl. "Where's the pasture that we're going to?"

Esteban pointed straight ahead. "About a half hour that way."

"I'll be back," she said, and whirled Athena around.

"June, wait," Esteban said.

But Athena had her orders. They thundered down the dirt path. June kept low in the saddle and let her girl fly. After she'd spent all the pent-up energy, Athena slowed down to a comfortable gallop.

Frenchie and Bob were surprised to see her.

"Gave up already?" Frenchie said and held out his hand to Bob. "Pay up. I told you she wouldn't last until lunch."

June felt his words like a gut punch. "Keep your money, Bob. I only came back for some work gloves and a spare shovel." If Esteban was going to test her, she was going to make sure she was damned prepared. Once she got her stuff, she rode hard until she saw the tail end of Esteban and his horse. Catching up to him was easy.

"You shouldn't work your horse that way," he said.

Still stinging from Frenchie's words, she snapped, "I know my horse's limitations. I've only been working with horses since I was sixteen freaking years old."

If Esteban was smart, he would leave it there. But of course, he was a man. And he had to explain to her how wrong she was. "Athena's built for speed, not endurance."

That was it. She had been looking for a fight ever since she got out of rehab. This would do just fine. "And how do you know what my horse is capable of?" But before he could open his mouth to say anything else, she went right on speaking. "And correct me if I'm wrong, but while we're digging and hammering in posts, our horses are going to be grazing for a few hours, right?"

The tips of Esteban's ears turned red. He was embarrassed? Good. Maybe he bet on her not lasting until lunch, too.

"Not only am I going to last until lunch, I'm going to out-dig, out-hammer, and out-repair you."

"It's not a contest," he said tightly.

"The hell it's not. You've got Vegas odds back in the bunkhouse on when I'm going to go crying back to Emily that I can't take the back-breaking labor."

"Wait, what?"

"Don't play dumb. Frenchie bet I was going to cash in before lunch. All I want to know is do I get to keep the money if I outlast all your bets?"

"That's bullshit. I'm sorry they did that. It's their asses as soon as I get a hold of them. Was it Frenchie and Bob, or everyone?" His jaw was set and June was surprised to see that he was really angry.

That stopped her cold. She had been ranting in frustration and venting. Esteban wasn't playing around.

"Look, it's okay."

"The hell it is," Esteban snarled. "We don't haze our new ranch hands and we certainly don't make bets on them. The fact that you're a woman puts the ranch in liability of a sexual harassment lawsuit."

"I'm certainly not going to sue Emily. She's my best friend," June said.

"It doesn't matter if you're going to or not. It matters that you could, and you'd have a case. Nate will address this tonight at dinner. I can promise you, it won't happen again."

This time when they rode in silence, June's mind was going a mile a minute. "Hey, I might have overreacted. It's what I do. I go off like a grenade, but then I'm fine."

"I'm kind of disappointed you're not wearing your Bad Attitude hat today."

"It's Bad Reputation, although I can see how you could make the mistake."

Esteban was still angry. She could see it in the hard set of his shoulders and how he gripped his reins. "I'm sorry you had to ride back. I should have checked with you before we left."

"Yeah, you should have."

But then she realized she had to take ownership of that as well. "I should have asked, though, if I needed any other supplies. I was just too eager to get started."

He gave a curt nod.

They had reached the pasture where they were going to work this morning. Athena was happy to graze with Esteban's horse. June knew from experience that if she did decide to wander off, a sharp whistle would bring her back.

Esteban explained what they needed to do, pointing to where she could find the posts and the wires. "Have you done this before?"

Resisting the urge to lie, she came clean. "Not this type of fencing, but I got it. If I have questions, I'll ask."

"Watch me do the first one."

Every instinct in her wanted to bristle and jump in that she could do it. But this wasn't a competition. Not anymore. At least not with Esteban. So she watched and learned how Esteban wanted it done.

"Now, it's your turn," she said. "Watch me and tell me if I'm doing it right or if there's a better way."

"Go ahead," he said.

He gave her a few pointers on how to use her knees more to lessen the strain on her back and shoulders. Soon they fell into an easy rhythm and June realized she didn't mind the quiet as much. When Esteban called for a break, June was proud of what she'd accomplished. Wetting her bandana with the water, she wiped off her face and neck, before tying it around her neck to keep her cool. She had serious hat head, but she was glad for the protection from the sun.

A pavilion had been set up with two chairs under the screened tent. She sat down, wondering if that was a good idea. She might not want to get up again. Esteban handed her two ibuprofen. "Take these now and save yourself a world of hurt later."

"Thanks." She swallowed them down, finishing the water in her water bottle. She refilled hers and Esteban's from the gallon jug that had been in his horse's saddlebags. Her eyelids drifted closed. Her snore woke her up and she bolted up, the chair flying back.

"I wasn't sleeping," June said, horrified.

Esteban smirked. "No, ma'am."

"Let's just get back to work."

"Whatever you say."

It was much slower going after their break. The sun was getting hotter and June was regretting the extra hour and a half less sleep she'd had this morning. "I've got to ask Janice if I can use good old number three again. The commute is going to kill me."

"No need. You can stay in the bunkhouse. I'll move in with Frenchie and you can take my room. Nate already arranged for it."

"I hate to be so predictable," she said, placing her hands on her hips. "I can't put you out."

"It's up to you." He shrugged. "But when Nate sets his mind to something, it's a done deal."

"Well, thank you." June frowned. She didn't want to be such a hassle. "I'm a pain in the ass, aren't I?"

Esteban's lips twitched. "I've only known you a few weeks. I'm not qualified to make that decision."

"My sisters will vouch for me. I feel bad for taking your room."

"Don't be. It's a glorified closet. But it does have its own bathroom and the door locks. Not that you'll have any trouble with the boys. They're good guys. Very loyal. They don't have anything against you. In fact, as you saw last night, they've followed your career, as well as Merry's, for a while now. Their current assholery will wear off soon."

They finished up the repairs on the fence quicker than she had expected. She was going to see if she could squeeze in a nap during lunch.

"You did a good job," Esteban said, looking at the new fence posts and the section they'd repaired.

"I had a good teacher," she said. "Are you surprised?"

"A bit." He nodded. "I had you pegged for a soft party girl."

"Guilty as charged."

"I wondered how you would do out here on your first day. I imagine Nate did too, otherwise he'd have put you mucking out the stalls."

"If he thought that was going to scare me off, he hasn't been paying attention. Does he think I have a butler who cleans out Athena's stall?"

"About that. I don't want to pry…"

"No, I don't have a butler. Merry and I take turns shoveling the shit," she said exasperated.

"You couldn't flirt your way into getting some empty-headed fanboy to do it for you?"

"No one goes near my horse that I don't know and trust." June's thoughts flickered back to Shayna James. If she'd shock her own horse, what would Shayna do to a rival's horse? The thought made her clench her fists. She'd better stay the hell away from Merry's Raphael.

"Easy there. I just wanted to know something that we've all been thinking about."

"Go ahead. I won't answer anything I don't want to."

"How long are you here for?" He held up a hand when she took a deep breath to let him have it. "The only gambling I do is poker. This isn't about a stupid bet. It's about my brother."

"Luis?"

"My other brother. His twin. Sam was going to be offered the next ranch hand position. I just want to know if this is a temporary thing so I can tell him to hang on. Or if you're in this for the long haul and he should look elsewhere."

Well, that explained the stink-eye Luis had given her.

"Hell, Esteban. I steal your brother's job, I kick you out of your room, I pick a fight with you on your first day… Why are you even still talking to me?"

Esteban looked down at his feet and then looked up at her. "Probably because I'm half in love with you. That's the other reason why I'm asking if you're going to stick around."

She could only gape at him while he put away the gear and prepared to ride out to the chuck wagon.

He'd said the "L" word. It didn't matter if he'd qualified it. The "L" word terrified her.

# Chapter Thirteen

I T WAS HARD not to keep defaulting back to resentment. In his head, Esteban knew June didn't set out to steal his brother's job, kick him out of his solo room, and then refuse to answer his question about whether or not she was going to stay at the ranch for a while. That didn't change the fact that she was doing all three.

They were the first to arrive at the chuck wagon, so it fell on them to help the Sullivans set up for lunch. As usual, Frank was there. His heart problems kept him off a horse, but nothing would stop him from driving the truck out to the lunch spots every day. Emily was there too, probably to help them out since Kelly shouldn't be hauling things around in this heat. But most likely, she was there to check up on June.

Once the folding tables and chairs were set up, they piled the coolers and trays of food on top. Today was sandwich day with fresh sub rolls and pound after pound of lunch meat with all the fixings. And because Emily was involved, there was also a tray of grilled vegetables, which to be honest, looked damned good. All they were waiting for was the rest of the crew to straggle in.

Frank grilled him on what the ranch hands were doing today, even though Nate must have let him know the plans.

"Where the hell are they? I'm ready to eat," Frank grumbled.

Esteban squinted into the distance, but didn't see any riders on the horizon. He checked his watch. "They still have ten minutes."

"Well, I'm starting without them." Frank began building his plate with the makings of a colossal sandwich.

"You're the boss," Esteban said.

"Frank, you shouldn't be having that much ham. Replace at least half of that with the vegetables your daughter made."

Frank shook his head at his wife and arched a look at him. "Yeah, I'm the boss all right." He did what he was told and then went to sit on the back of the truck to eat.

June and Emily sat under the large pop-up pavilion tent with their iced teas, waiting for the crew to arrive. Esteban stuck to Sarah's magical lemonade and tried not to eavesdrop on their conversation. From what he could hear, they were talking about the feud between Merry and Shayna James and how Merry had promised to be back in time for Emily's wedding next week.

A part of him was hoping June would spout out her opinions about marriage because the argument between her and Emily would be fun to watch. But June behaved herself.

Or at least, she tried to. He caught her looking at him when she thought he wouldn't notice. He probably should have kept the fact that he was falling in love with her to himself, at least until he found out if she felt the same. But it was better to get it out sooner rather than later. He didn't have to hide that he was looking at her. Unfortunately, not only did Emily notice and leaned into whisper something into June's ear that made her giggle, but Sarah also noticed.

"She's a firecracker, that one," Sarah said, handing him a bag of ice to add to the trays under the fruit salad. The potato salad and butter were still sealed in deep-freeze coolers until the ranch hands came in. There was no need to worry about spoiling—both would vanish in minutes.

"I can't believe she's here," he said.

"She's different," Sarah said. "At times like this, there's no trace of the wild girl she pretends to be."

"I don't know about that. She rode her horse naked down Main Street because she was bored. Do you think she'll stick around?" Esteban asked. He felt guilty about asking, but it didn't make a damn bit of sense. He was an average rider. He was a competent roper. But he couldn't stay on a bull or a horse that didn't want him there. As much as he wanted to run away with the rodeo when he was a kid, he knew it hadn't been in the cards for him. But if it had been, he would have gone and never looked back. In his gut, he knew it was just a matter of time before June went back, but he didn't want her to go.

"I don't know. It's driving Frank nuts because he likes her and hopes she settles down here."

He could relate. But there wasn't time to dwell on it. The rest of the ranch hands were riding toward the chuck wagon.

After everyone piled food high on their plates, June made it a point to sit with the ranch hands instead of going back under the tent with Emily.

"Shove over, Ringo," she said, throwing a long leg over the bench.

Ringo lifted up and scooted over a half inch.

June scowled at him. "I said move, dumbass."

Ringo moved. "Jeez, you don't have to be such a bitch."

Sarah frowned. Esteban headed over to explain to Ringo how he felt about that word, when June just snorted and said, "Takes one to know one."

The laughter around the table cleared out any of the tension, but it still left Esteban feeling like he needed to drive his fist into Ringo's face.

Nate's hand fell heavy on his shoulder and he had to check himself from whirling on his boss.

"Good job finishing the Firecracker fence," Nate said.

Frank Sullivan named all of his pastures after famous bulls.

"I took a ride by to see your progress," Nate added, seeing Esteban's questioning look.

So that was why they had all been late to lunch. Everyone must have done the same thing. It got his back up and he glowered at the ranch hands who were too busy stuffing their faces to notice.

"I need a second opinion on Lonestar's shoe." Nate steered him away from the table and over to where the horses were.

That was a bullshit excuse. The day Nate couldn't tell if

his horse had something in his shoe would be the day he'd hang it up for good. But it got them out of earshot of the peanut gallery.

"How did she do?" Nate asked gesturing to June with his chin.

"Fine," Esteban bit out. But as he looked over, it looked like she was really dragging it. Normally, if had been one of the guys, Esteban would have suggested to Nate to give them afternoon farm duty and have them help out with the animals at the ranch. But he was afraid that if he suggested that, it would diminish all of June's hard work today.

On the other hand, he didn't want her collapsing, face first, in the middle of the pasture.

"She's working out, but she needs to be in the bunkhouse so she's not dead on her feet by noon. She's willing to move in. I can have everything out of my room by tonight. And maybe she can pack an overnight bag until her day off when she can move in properly."

"I think we can do it even faster than that." Nate cupped his hand by his mouth so his voice amplified. "June, come here a minute."

She scrambled up and dumped her plate and utensils into the wash bin. "What's going on?" She glared up at Nate when she joined them by the horses.

"Do you have a problem with sharing the bunkhouse with six men?"

June's eyes lit up with mischief. Esteban shook his head at her, minutely, to warn her off baiting Nate.

"I think the question is if they have a problem with me?"

"They don't. And if they do, then they have a problem with *me*." Nate jerked his thumb to his chest.

Esteban could tell that June wanted to argue with Nate, but even she seemed to realize that she would be arguing just for the sake of arguing, and gave in gracefully. "That would be a big help to me in the mornings. I've shared close quarters before while traveling to the rodeos across the country. I won't have a problem."

"If you feel unsafe, all you have to do is let Emily, Esteban or me know."

"I can take care of myself," she said, her chin going up.

"I never thought you couldn't. But you don't have to." Nate looked at Esteban. "Keep them in line."

"Got it."

"Good. After lunch, clean up the chuck wagon and go back to the bunkhouse. I want her moved in by dinner."

"Will do," Esteban said.

Nate went back to the table and took her seat next to Ringo. Not so surprisingly, there was plenty of room to sit at the table. June looked over Esteban. "Sorry to kick you out of your room."

"I told you once he makes up his mind, it happens."

"Still, it doesn't feel right."

"As long as it doesn't feel right because you're worried about my delicate feelings and not because you're afraid to live with six strange men."

"Five strange men and you."

Esteban tried to hide the smile on his face. "I would think, after what I said to you this morning, that you'd be worried about me the most."

"Was I that obvious?"

"I noticed you didn't say anything. Am I reading the signs wrong? I think we have something."

"We do, but I don't do the 'L' word."

Esteban nodded. "That's because you're chicken."

"I beg your pardon?"

"You like doing crazy things, right?"

June narrowed her eyes at him. "Right."

"What could be crazier than getting involved with me?"

"Crazy how?"

"Well, there's a lot going against us. For one, my brothers resent you."

She made a face at him. "I told you, I didn't know about Sam."

"That and my mother wasn't impressed with your naked ride down Main Street."

"To be fair, she wasn't my demographic."

"So what would be crazier than dating your supervisor whose family would…"

"Feed me to the pigs if they found out."

"I'm not sure they'd go that far, but you have to admit, it's a risk."

June smiled and looked around the camp. "We'd have to keep it a secret from all the other guys, too. Otherwise they'll think I slept my way into the job and that would go hard on you with them and your family."

"This is beginning to sound like a caper."

"More shenanigans than a caper, but you're not wrong."

"The big risk, though, is that you'll fall in love with me too."

Her eyes grew wide at the thought. "I don't want to hurt you."

"That's another risk—one I'm willing to take. Because I'm betting that at the end of this, you're not only going to be in love with me, but you're going to marry me, too."

"You are crazy," she said.

"But you're tempted," he said, feigning nonchalance that he didn't feel. "You're worried that I'm going to change your mind about marriage."

"I'm not worried at all," she said and gave him a slow once-over that made him wish they were alone.

"So, are we doing this?" Esteban asked.

"Okay, assholes," Nate said, standing up and talking to the ranch hands. "June is taking Esteban's room and Esteban's moving in with Frenchie. Get used to shifting beds around, since sooner or later, we're going to be hiring four more hands."

At that moment, Sarah sweetened Nate's announcement by coming out with a batch of cherry tartlets. Between Nate's death glare and the pastries, there wasn't a lot of grumbling.

The fact that Frank was there too—and he obviously adored June—also kept any complaining to a minimum.

"Maybe," June answered him, sending him a coy look before going to grab a cherry tartlet before they were all gone.

Esteban could work with maybe.

"That horse of yours sure is a beauty," Frank said, after the ranch hands rode out to start their afternoon chores.

"I don't know what I would've done without her," June said, giving Athena an affectionate rub. "She's the whole reason I won all those championships."

Frank guffawed. "I've seen the way you and your sister Merry ride. You could've had ridden Clydesdales and come out on top."

"You're good for my ego," she said, helping him slide the last few tables and chairs into the back of the pickup truck.

"So how long are you going to be with us?" Frank asked.

That was the magic question. Esteban was curious to hear her answer.

"I'm here for the long run," she said.

He had mixed feelings about that. He wanted her to be here with him while they further developed their relationship, but he also knew this wasn't what she wanted to do with her life.

"What's going on with you and the rodeo?" Frank asked.

Esteban had to admire the old man. He was like a dog worrying a bone.

Cocking her head to the side, she thought about his question for a long minute. "I'm taking some time off."

"If you don't mind me asking..." Frank said.

"And even if you do," Sarah interrupted. "He'll ask anyway."

June smiled. "Go ahead. Hit me with it."

"Why on earth would you give up a life like that, for a life like this?"

"Emily said she needed help and I couldn't refuse." She smiled and left it at that.

She was good at stopping people from getting too close. He was glad she had trusted him with her secret. June had to have known that it was going to get out eventually, but for the time being at least, her rehab stint and her troubles with the WPRC were still not common knowledge.

They rode back to the ranch and put their horses away. Esteban grabbed a few boxes and garbage bags. He was only moving down the hall, so he didn't need much to transport his stuff. He had given Frenchie the heads-up last night that this might happen, and Frenchie had moved his shit to one side of the room already, just in case.

June looked around the inside of the bunkhouse. "It seems cozy."

"Last chance to change your mind," he said as they walked into his room.

"If I was a man and I took on this job, I would be staying here. It's only been one day, and I can tell you right now getting up an hour and a half early every day is not going to make me an efficient worker. Not to mention, I'll be a total bitch. And while I take pride in my bitchiness, I don't like to take it out on people who don't deserve it. This ranch deserves my best. I need this job. I only wish that I didn't have to kick you out of your bunk in order to get a room here. I was more than happy to rent a room from Janice."

Esteban started emptying his drawers and shoving the contents into the garbage bag. "Yeah, the only problem with that is Janice's retreats are usually sold out. And she doesn't have that many rooms to begin with. Trust me, you'd rather stay at the bunkhouse than stay at the retreat center when Charlie Lincoln and his prison boys come around."

"Prison boys?"

"Charlie is quite the character. He's Donovan's father. Remember I told you about him? He's an ex-con who is now working to help other ex-cons rehabilitate into society. But they're all white-collar criminals, so you don't have to worry about being murdered in your sleep."

"That's good," June said.

"His group rents out the retreat center twice a month. Poker night is banging when he's up. Between him and Cole Lockwood, you won't have a cent left in your paycheck. One of these days, I'll beat them both. But not anytime in the near future."

June walked into the bathroom. "Hey, do you mind if I take a shower? I can't stand myself."

"Uh sure." He wondered if that was a not so subtle hint that he stunk as well.

"Great, thanks." She shut the door and he heard the shower start.

It probably wouldn't kill him to take one as well. "I'm going to shower too. I'll be right back."

She didn't answer him. Since they were the only ones in the bunkhouse, he stripped as he walked to his new room, making a pit stop to dump his dirty clothes into the empty washer. He'd wait until after June's shower to start the machine up.

It felt like a luxury to take a shower midday and he took

longer than he usually did. When he got out with just a towel around his waist, he nearly walked into the wall in shock when he saw June standing by the washer trying to figure out how it worked.

She had her hair bundled up into one of those towel turbans, and she was wearing one of his T-shirts. It hit her mid-thigh, but the fact that she was naked under it stopped him dead in his tracks. He needed to get it together.

But she noticed him first. "Hey, cowboy, come here often?" She slanted him a sultry look.

"Not as often as I like," his mouth said before his brain could stop it.

"That's a shame. Can you show me how to start this up? My clothes walked down here by themselves and threw themselves in."

He never thought that showing someone how to use the washer could be erotic...until now. "You toss the pod in, select the load and just hit start."

"Great." She closed the lid and the old machine rattled to life. "Now that looks like a good time." Hoisting herself up to sit on top of the machine, June tugged down her shirt. But he got a flash of long legs and creamy thighs before he remembered to look away. "Oooh, this feels like riding the Harley one of my boyfriends had."

Esteban couldn't look at her. He cleared his throat. "You're probably not going to want to do that when the guys are here. In fact, it might be best for you to do your clothes separately."

"That's a waste of water," she purred. "We're doing ours

together, aren't we?"

He finally looked at her. "Are you trying to drive me crazy?"

She laughed. "Is it working?"

"A bit. Now get down from there before you give me a heart attack."

June eased down to her feet and toweled off her long hair before opening the washer up and tossing the towel in.

He wanted her. He was painfully hard just being so close to her and smelling his soap on her skin.

"Let's get you packed," she said. "And then we can go to my mama's trailer and pick up my things."

Esteban watched her wiggle back to his bedroom. He wasn't sure how he was going to keep his hands off her.

JUNE WASN'T SURE how she was going to keep her hands off him. She wanted to yank that towel right off him. She was feeling sexy with the smell of his soap and clothes all over her. And the vibrations of the washing machine had kicked her hormones into overdrive.

"I should get dressed," he said, but didn't move.

"Should you?" she asked, sitting on the bed. It was narrow, but big enough for both of them.

Esteban took in a sharp breath. "Are you trying to seduce me?"

"Why not? I know it's not the hotel room I promised, but it's here and now instead of next weekend." June was going to prove to him that it was just a sex thing and not an "L" word thing.

Esteban's eyes hooded. "If we do this, we're a thing. You're my woman and I'm your man."

"Exclusive doesn't work for me. I've tried it before and gotten burned." June looked away. She did not want to think about Dustin right now.

He sat down on the bed next to her. His shoulder grazed hers and she trembled. This would be easier if she didn't want him so damned much.

"I'm not like other guys."

That was true.

"There's no one else for me."

She swallowed. "Do you always fall in love so fast?"

"No. The girls I dated weren't right for me. You're different."

Esteban was sexy enough to make her toes curl under normal circumstances, but if he didn't kiss her, like right this minute, June was sure she was going to explode.

"Who hurt you, June?" he asked, softly touching her cheek.

"He doesn't matter."

"I'm glad to hear that. Because if he doesn't matter, I want a chance." He nuzzled her cheek. "I thought you liked to take chances."

"I don't think your family is ever going to like me," she said.

"They don't have to. But it is a challenge I'm sure you're up to." Esteban hooked a finger into the collar of the T-shirt she was wearing and kissed her shoulder.

"This is crazy," she said with a shaky sigh.

"It is," he murmured. "It's too soon. Too fast." He turned her chin to him and finally, *finally* kissed her.

*Yes!* She had missed having his mouth on hers.

"It's perfect," he said, after a long kiss that left her needing more. "We don't have much time, pretty girl. Are you mine or not?"

"Kiss me again and I'll think about it."

He pushed her back on the bed and climbed in next to her. He kissed softly and her body rolled closer to his. Reaching down, she undid the towel around his hip and wrapped her leg over him.

There were plenty of crazy things she could do in her spare time. She could take up skydiving or learn how to pilot a hot-air balloon. Neither of those things would break her heart.

Neither of those things would make her feel like this.

"Well?" he asked, breathless from kissing her senseless.

"I want a lot of sex," June negotiated.

"Good."

"The minute you want someone else, you let me know. I don't want to walk in on you or find out from someone else."

"Not going to happen, but okay, I promise."

Something tight within her loosened.

"I'm not the marrying type," she warned.

Esteban set his jaw. "The minute you want someone else, you let me know. The same rules apply."

June didn't see that happening, but she would end this before it did. "Done. Same goes if your family makes it difficult for you when they find out about us."

"I think we're getting somewhere." Esteban pulled the T-shirt up and over her head.

"Last thing, we keep this between you and me so the ranch hands and Nate don't think the wrong thing," she said.

He held out his pinkie. "Pinkie promise."

"What?" June chuckled. "Are we twelve?"

"I have it on good authority this is the strongest vow."

She curled her pinkie around his. "Pinkie promise."

"Say you're mine," he said.

She took a deep breath. This was crazy. This was wild. This was exciting. And he was right. This felt perfect. High stakes. High risks.

"I'm yours," she said, the words easier to say than she thought they'd be.

"And I'm yours," he murmured, skimming his fingertips over her pebbled nipples.

The thundercloud of dread that had been overhead for the past four months suddenly lifted. She smoothed her hands over the hard muscles of his arms. "You're so damned sexy. Even when you're being annoying."

"Took the words right out of my mouth, darlin'."

Kissing him was better than sex with anyone else, especially when they were naked. She reached down to stroke him and he moaned into her mouth.

"Esteban," she whispered. "I want you." Her hips

twitched.

"Good."

Dipping his fingers inside her, he tickled her clit as she rubbed him faster. Their kisses became more frantic, more frenzied. He pulled her head away from his, tugging on her hair, which just made her wetter. "I'm going to come all over you if you don't stop."

"I'm not stopping," she gritted out.

"Then look at me when you come. Don't you look away." His fingers were lightning fast and she matched him stroke for stroke. Enchanted by what she saw in his eyes, she leaned in so the tips of her nipples brushed against his. He exploded over both of them with a tortured shout. Hot and thick and primitive, the noises he made as she tugged on him were music to her ears.

His eyes were lustful and tortured. And then it was her turn to cry out. She turned her head and sank her teeth into his shoulder. Esteban growled possessively and clamped his hand on her ass.

Flipping her over on her hands and knees, he reached for a condom in his bedside table. She watched him over her shoulder, shivering in anticipation. After fitting it on, he drove into her and her entire body locked around him.

"Are you coming again?" he chuckled.

"Move damn you," she grated out. "Hard. Fast."

Always the gentleman, Esteban obliged and she wailed and writhed at each thrust of his body that plunged his wide, hot cock into her.

"More," she moaned as he relentlessly drilled into her.

The bedsprings creaked like they were coming apart and the headboard slammed against the wall hard enough to make dents. His lustful grunts pushed her closer to the edge and his driving body gave her endless waves of friction-filled pleasure. June came and just held on as waves and waves of it crashed over her, until it was his turn to come again, shaking and panting.

Esteban collapsed on her. Pushing aside her hair, he whispered in her ear, "You're amazing."

"What the hell just happened?" she asked, breathing hard.

"We made a mess." He chuckled and then scooped her up as if she weighed nothing. "And there's no more hot water so this is going to be cold and quick." He set her on her feet and joined her in the shower. Then he turned on the arctic blast.

June cursed him with every swear word she knew. But to his credit, he washed them both off quickly and then turned off the water. He toweled her dry, rubbing warmth into her.

"You've got quite the vocabulary," he said, kissing her neck.

Closing her eyes, she clung to him. She wanted more of him. Not just now, but tomorrow and the day after and she wasn't sure how they were going to manage that in a houseful of other men. This was scary and risky, not because she was afraid of being caught—that had its own kinky appeal—but of the way he made her feel. She didn't want to be without him, or this feeling she belonged to him.

Hopping up, she wrapped her legs around him and he

walked them back to the bed and under the covers to warm up. June wasn't tongue-tied too often, but she wasn't sure what to say. Would he even still want her now that she had given in and handed him everything? That was the crazy risk she took.

Esteban stroked a hand lazily up her spine and she cuddled into him like a kitten as her eyes drifted shut. She was dimly aware of him kissing her eyelids and forehead. It was a tender gesture that twisted her heart, but before she could figure out why, she was asleep.

# Chapter Fourteen

E STEBAN DIDN'T HAVE the heart to wake June up. She slept through him moving out. Slept through him unpacking in Frenchie's room. She was still out when he brought her clean clothes back to her from the dryer and when he folded them and put them away, along with the T-shirt of his that she'd swiped.

He thought about waking her, but they would totally be busted, especially with her hair a snarly wet mess. Instead, he tucked the blanket closer around her. Turning over on her stomach, she started to snore. He thought she was adorable. And he wanted her again, wanted her mouth on him, and wanted her riding his cock.

Closing his eyes, he struggled to get a grip. Reluctantly, he locked the door behind him, just in case someone decided to get nosy. She could leave, but no one could get in.

As it was, it was a good call not to wake her up. As soon as he stepped foot out on the porch, he saw the ranch hands trickling in, led by Nate.

"Is she all moved in?" Nate asked as he joined them in the barn to help with the horses.

Esteban rolled his eyes and pretended to be exasperated.

"She's still got another truckload of stuff at her mama's, but she said she'd get the rest later."

"Where is she now?"

Esteban shrugged. "I don't know. I'm assuming still putting things away. I was going to head into town for some beer—we're getting low."

"Get a couple of bottles of red wine for tonight. Something spicy to go with my meatballs," Tony said.

"I'll get whatever's on sale," Esteban said.

"Heathen." Frenchie glowered at him. "Leave the wine to me. You stick with the beer."

And just like that, he managed to get away without anyone asking what he and June had been up to this afternoon.

JUNE DIDN'T COME down for dinnertime. He crept up to check on her and she was still snoring her pretty little head off.

"She's sleeping," he said after coming back down to report that June wouldn't be joining them.

"I can't believe she lasted the day," Frenchie said.

"About that..." Esteban stood in the middle of the common room, blocking the television. He glared them all down when they started to bitch about him being a better door than a window. "The bets you have going on? It ends tonight."

"Aw, Esteban, we're just having fun," Bob said.

"Knock it off or I'll take it to Nate. Then you can explain to him why you're being a dick to the owner's best friend."

"She'd tattle like a little girl?" Ringo asked with a sneer.

"No, and I don't think she'd file a sexual harassment suit either. But you guys are asking for one."

"I knew having a woman around would change everything. I bet I can't even fart without it causing a scandal," Bob said.

"I think we'd all appreciate you not letting go indoors, at least." Esteban rubbed his hand down his face.

"What about you?" Frenchie asked.

Esteban was pretty sure he wasn't talking about passing wind. "If you got something to say, come out and say it."

"You're a sexual harassment suit waiting to happen. Technically, you're her boss and you're following her around like a lovesick puppy."

"What would Sam say?" Luis asked.

Unclenching his jaw took a lot of effort. He refused to rise to the bait. They didn't know shit. He kept up the lie. "I helped her move her stuff after a long day. That's all. It's called being a team player and a decent human being." But their words stung all the same.

Sam would be devastated that he'd jumped into bed with the woman who stole his job. It wouldn't matter if she hadn't planned to do it. It wouldn't matter to his brother, his pregnant girlfriend, or their mother. But that hadn't been June's fault.

"Look, I know you're all just being loyal to Sam and me, and I appreciate that. But we've got to give June a chance.

You know as well as I do that we need more than one person around here. Once June's settled in, maybe we can ask her to put in a good word with Emily."

"Fine, now get out of the way," Bob said.

Esteban wasn't about to beat a dead horse, so he moved. He wasn't ready to sit down and watch *Jeopardy* with them, though. He was feeling restless, as if ants were crawling all over him. He could bring his dinner to his room and read or stare at his phone until exhaustion took him, but he didn't think that would help. He wanted June. He wanted to fall asleep next to her.

He walked outside and took a deep breath of the fresh night air. The sun had set an hour ago. Esteban liked this time of night the best, when the shadows took on an air of magic and menace. He wished June was here to share dinner with him. He wanted to talk to her. When it was quiet like this, it ate at him that his family would think he was betraying them for falling in love with June.

He saw the lights were still on at the main house, and in Nate and Janice's cabin. Without consciously deciding to, he headed over that way, but when he got too close, a cacophony of barking dogs broke the silence of the night.

Janice peeked her head out the door.

"I'm so sorry for causing all that," he said.

"If it wasn't you, it would have been an armadillo. Do you want to come in?"

"I don't want to intrude. I was wondering if I could speak to Nate for a bit?"

"Sure. Nate!" She hollered over the din of the dogs.

"Esteban's here."

A few minutes later, Nate sidled out of the door with Daisy, his Australian sheepdog at his heels. "I was expecting you'd come around."

"I don't mean to be a pain in the ass, but I was wondering if you had a chance to speak to Emily and ask her about hiring Sam."

"Let's walk," Nate said, whistling for Daisy to follow. They headed over to the bocce court that Frank had raked over and set aside. Esteban knew the game as *petanque.* The throwing techniques were different, but the game was basically the same. It involved tossing a small ball called a *pallino* to start the game, and then seeing who could get the closest by chucking their larger, heavier boules underhand. Frank had learned it while he was recovering from his heart attack. The rehabilitation unit had taught it to a bunch of the older gentlemen, but then had to stop the program because of how agitated they were getting over the scoring.

Esteban was more of a horseshoes man, himself. There was a pit set up for that as well. "Care for a game?" he asked Nate.

"If you're in the mood to get your ass kicked, I'll oblige you." Nate flicked on the spotlights that illuminated the court areas. Squatting down, he handed Nate a set of shoes with the ends tinged in blue. He chose the red-edged ones for himself. They did a few practice throws before getting into the game in earnest. Esteban knew enough not to rush Nate, so he enjoyed the game and concentrated on getting a ringer on the stake.

"Emily isn't opposed to hiring another hand," Nate said when they were measuring the distance of the horseshoes to the pin to see who won. Daisy circled around them now that it was safe from flying metal objects.

A flare of hope surged inside Esteban, even as he heard the yet unspoken "but."

"But she needs to be a little conservative with the hiring. I suspect Sam will be hired by the end of the year, but I can't get more specific than that."

"I get it," he said. And he did. It still gave him a vicious pleasure that he beat his boss in horseshoes, though. And that he might be able to enjoy June on the down-low until Sam got hired and they could come out to everyone about their relationship. It didn't sit well with him to keep her a secret. He wanted everyone to know that June Grayson was his.

"Want a beer?" Nate asked when they got back to the house.

"No, I should be winding down. We've got a long day ahead of us tomorrow."

"I haven't even told you what we're going to be doing."

"Well, they're all long days."

Nate grunted. "You got that right. But we're going to move the herd at Asteroid to Bushwacker. I want you to keep an eye out on June."

"I plan on it. But do you think there's going to be trouble? She did all right today." He had to admit, June had surprised him. She admitted when she needed help and took direction well.

"She's not used to working with a team. It's always been just her, and maybe her sister too. I can see the chip on her shoulder a mile away and I don't care what put it there. I don't want her getting hurt or getting someone else hurt because she's grandstanding instead of being a team player."

"She can ride and rope and has the trophies to prove it." Esteban had to be careful he didn't give himself away. He was soft in the head when it came to her. Even now, he wondered if he could sneak back into his old room and wake her with kisses.

No. It was impossible. And he had to get that through his head. They couldn't have sex in the bunkhouse again. Fortunately, his mind reminded him that next week was the wedding and he'd have all weekend to be with her, far away from the ranch.

"Yeah. I'm not confident in her ability to take orders without an argument or doing something the way I want it done and not the way she thinks it should be done. Until that happens, make sure she doesn't see the side of my temper that's going to get her and me in a boatload of trouble."

"I'm on it," Esteban said, giving him a half wave. Great, now he was babysitter, too.

When Esteban got back to the bunkhouse, he still wasn't ready to face sharing a room with Frenchie. Against his better judgment, he got into his truck and went for a drive. Last Stand was a small town and at ten o'clock at night, the sidewalks all but rolled themselves up. Still, there were a few people out and about. He waved as he passed Chief Highwater, who was sitting in his squad car keeping an eye on things.

He headed over to Buddy's Bar and Boogie in Whiskey River.

"One drink," he said to himself and then he'd head off to his cold and lonely bed…unless he could figure out a way to slip into June's without the entire bunkhouse knowing about it. Pushing away the seductive vision of both of them sharing his bed, Esteban parked his truck outside of the bar.

The rocking sound of country music coming from the jukebox inside put him in a festive mood. He couldn't wait until Emily and Donovan's wedding. Then, he could just be Esteban, not Sam's brother, not June's supervisor, just Esteban. And she could be just June, a pretty girl whose smile did crazy things to his libido.

Esteban nodded at a few people he knew and sat at the bar. The television above it was playing a WPRC event. Merry Grayson and Shayna James were competing for first place. He rooted for Merry out of loyalty to June, because it seemed to be cheating on June to root for his previous fantasy crush. Now that he looked at her though, he noticed that Shayna's appeal was that she resembled June a bit—she was a poor man's June Grayson. Esteban was more than happy to have the original. If he closed his eyes, he could feel June's hand on his cock and the taste of her in his mouth.

"Esteban." A hand clamped on his back hard and he nearly fell off the barstool.

"Oh hey, Charlie, how are you doing?"

Charlie Lincoln was a silver-haired version of his son—

not that Esteban would ever mention that to Donovan.

"Looking forward to our next retreat. You're going to love these guys. They're looking into getting jobs in ranching. I've got a call with Nate tomorrow to see if he's got some work for them to do while they're on our retreat. You get the free labor, and those bums get the experience. It'll be a win-win."

"Yeah," Esteban said sourly, taking a pull of his beer. While he was glad for the extra help—and Emily would jump at the chance at free labor—it pushed off Sam's hiring date. Why pay for a hand when every month or so, Charlie brought in a team?

"Is it true that April's sister is working at the ranch?"

"Yup," Esteban drawled. News traveled fast.

Charlie whistled. "It's good to have friends in high places. She's lucky Emily took her in."

Esteban decided not to engage. Charlie obviously wanted to talk, though, so there was no getting rid of him until he'd said his piece. Cracking open a couple of peanuts from the bowl in front of him, Esteban watched Merry take a tight turn and head into the stall in record time.

"Heh, Merry's good. But June's better. June's lucky she's not in jail. She got a sympathetic judge who let her do rehab time instead."

He couldn't let that slide. "You probably shouldn't start rumors like that." He concentrated on opening up a few more peanuts so Charlie didn't know just how damned pissed off he was.

"It's the truth. I've got friends on the circuit and they

told me how it all went down. 'Bad Reputation' June Grayson, drunk off her ass, got into the mother of all catfights with 'Girl Next Door' Shayna James. She cut off Shayna's ponytail and Shayna beat the ever-loving shit out of her."

That was a hell of a story. June hadn't mentioned that, but it could have been the reason why she wasn't back on the circuit. She had mentioned that a PR guy had said to Trent that he didn't want June associated in any way with the WPRC. Esteban couldn't see the catfight between her and Shayna though. "June doesn't seem like the type. She's a party girl, sure, but nothing she's ever done pointed to her being a violent drunk."

"Shayna stole June's man."

A flash of jealousy hit him low and unexpected. "Who?" he snarled.

"Who else?" Charlie pointed up at the screen. "Dustin Greaves, the men's champion. My friends say Dustin and June were engaged."

"Engaged?" Esteban choked out, all pretense that he wasn't interested forgotten. That kiss she and Dustin shared that went viral all over social media suddenly made sense. Was it really a kiss goodbye to piss off Shayna? Or had that rekindled the flame?

"Yup. Word is she caught Shayna and Dustin banging in her trailer. Boom! They fight. The WPRC sent Shayna to mandatory anger management classes and June got sentenced to three months in rehab to dry out and get her shit together. And now she's hiding out at the Three Sisters licking her wounds, while her sister's been working her ass off to keep Shayna James from winning another title."

"But she's out of rehab now. Why isn't she back in the arena?" Esteban asked, playing dumb. He wondered if Charlie knew the PR guy who had blacklisted June.

"Apparently, Shayna makes for a more wholesome champion than our own Grayson sisters."

"So this is all a con, a show for the folks at home, but the winner has already been decided on?" Esteban scoffed.

"I know you're a betting man, but I wouldn't bet that Merry wins the barrel-racing championship."

"If word got out that the races are fixed, Shayna wouldn't be the girl next door anymore, would she?"

"Rumor has it, Shayna's looking to ditch that reputation. That's why she stole June's man out from under her. But my friends in the rodeo say that Shayna's bridezilla ways are alienating Dustin. It's only a matter of time before we get a fairy-tale scene with Prince Charming coming to the Three Sisters Ranch to bring the Rodeo Queen back into the fold."

Esteban gripped his bottle tight enough that he heard the glass give. Forcing himself to remove a finger one at a time, he wiped his hand on his jeans. "That so?" he said with a casual tone he didn't come close to feeling. "Good thing my brother Sam is ready to take her place."

"If she has a brain in her head, she won't take him back. But if she's anything like her mama, she'll run to him with open arms. I'll look into it more, if you're interested."

"I'm interested," Esteban said. "Do you know anything about a PR guy named Sinclair?"

"No, but I could ask my friends what they know." Charlie leaned forward. "Why?"

"He's got a grudge against June, and I want to know why."

"Do you think it will affect the ranch?" Charlie asked.

Esteban sipped on his beer. "It might."

# Chapter Fifteen

HER FIRST WEEK as a ranch hand could have gone better, but it wasn't a total shit storm either. June had made a few mistakes, but had owned up to them. She still couldn't shake the feeling that they were all waiting for her to screw up and that they were talking about her behind her back. But she didn't have any proof of it.

Esteban went out of his way not to be alone with her all week. He texted her a few times, telling her that they had to be careful because Luis was watching them like a hawk. It was growing a little old and she decided that she didn't care who knew she was sleeping with Esteban. But she didn't want to make his job any harder, so she kept those feelings to herself. When she'd agreed to this situation, she didn't think it would be like this.

June hid her frustration by throwing herself into work. Eat, work, sleep. That's all she did. The two days she had off, she had to spend smuggling in her things so no one knew that she and Esteban had had mind-blowing sex instead of moving her in like they'd been supposed to.

She skipped out after Esteban's pozole dinner on Saturday, not even feeling a little bit guilty about not helping him clean up. She had to head over to Mama's and help her make three trays of lasagna for tomorrow's dinner.

June wasn't surprised to see her sister April waiting there for her at her mother's trailer.

"Where's Cole?" June asked. "I figured the two of you were still attached at the hip."

"He's working." April shrugged. "He still can't shake the need to work a couple of extra jobs to get ahead of the bills."

"I'll take that over the alternative, any day," Penny said. Their mother was still in her prime, even though she'd had more husbands than most people had pairs of shoes in her sixty years on earth.

"So, how may trays of lasagna do you think I'll need, Mama?" June asked.

"How many men have you got?"

"There are seven of us altogether."

Penny tilted her head to think about it. "Well, seven trays are probably the safest bet."

"Mama! That's a lot of lasagna."

"Well, for one meal, sure." Penny started laying the empty trays out on the table. "But you're going to want some extra for leftovers."

"No leftovers. They get breakfast, lunch, and dinner cooked for them every day."

"Yeah, but what about snack time?" Penny put a large pot on to boil.

"I still think that's a lot of food. I was thinking maybe three trays?"

"Honey, trust the expert. It's always better to have too

much than too little. Y'all have a freezer over there. Don't you?"

"Yes." It was currently stocked up with frozen beef.

"Then the worst thing that happens is you have next week's dinner already prepared."

June couldn't argue with that. As they waited for the large lasagna pasta noodles to cook, they sat at the table and cut sticks of pepperoni into little wheels and then into fourths so that they resembled little pieces of pies. Then they chopped the fresh mozzarella into little coins.

Penny grabbed a large skillet and browned the bulk sausage while June served them iced cold lemon seltzers. June gulped hers down and then refilled it. She wanted a glass of wine. It was going to be worse once Mama warmed up her homemade tomato sauce from the stash she had canned last summer.

"So how do you like working at the Three Sisters Ranch?" April asked. "Nate seems like he'd be a tough boss."

"He's all right." June shrugged and went up to get a twist of lime for her seltzer. Mama didn't have limes. Staring into the fridge, she tried to ignore the open bottle of wine in there. *Seriously, who has leftover wine?*

Probably someone who didn't have to go to rehab.

Sighing, June plunked back down at the table.

"But…?" April said, nudging her with an elbow.

June hadn't thought she was that transparent.

"But the rest of the guys haven't seemed to warm up to me yet," June admitted. And the one who did warm up to her was now going out of his way to avoid her.

"That's why you need this lasagna," Penny said. "Trust me. This will knock their socks off. Those ranch hands will be begging for more. And they'll have to be damned nice to you in order to get some."

"If we're really trying to bribe them, can April make her famous chocolate chip cookies, too?" June batted her eyelashes at her sister.

"Oh, when you put it like that," April said, fake swooning. "How can anyone ever resist you?"

It felt good to be home. While June was glad that she didn't have to wake up an hour and a half earlier every morning in order to hit the four a.m. chow time, she missed being around people she could talk to. After dinner, the ranch hands went to the common area to watch Sports Center, or back to their rooms. June enjoyed a good football game as much as the next girl, but she didn't feel comfortable sitting around with men she barely knew. She had hoped that Esteban would at least be there to help ease her into the social aspect of the job. Maybe play cards or a board game to break the ice with the rest of the hands, but that hadn't happened. Maybe if she could have a few beers with them, it would help her become part of the team, but she wasn't ready to do that yet.

"What do guys like?" June asked, drumming her fingers on the table.

"Sex," Penny said.

Been there, done that. Was in an exclusive relationship again. That still blew her mind.

Luckily the noodles were ready to be placed in the pans,

and June was able to put off that conversation. She was on ricotta duty. After every layer of sausage, pepperoni, and mozzarella cheese, June scooped in a few dollops of ricotta. They worked in companionable silence constructing the lasagnas.

"There," Penny said, dusting her hands off. "All that's left is for you to cook them. Do you want to bring them back to the bunkhouse and bake the trays tonight? I'll guarantee that you'll get hungry cowboys sniffing around wondering what's up."

"No," June said. "I'd rather stay here and cook them now, if you don't mind." That way all she had to do was warm them up.

"I don't mind at all. It's great to have both my girls here at the same time. If only Merry was here too, it would be like Christmas."

"How is Merry doing?" June asked. "I've barely been able to keep up with our text conversations. I don't have a lot of time to look at my phone during the day. And at night, I'm usually so tired, I go right to bed after dinner."

"You haven't missed much," April said. "Merry is working her butt off, trying to win every competition she can. I think she's just being vindictive now. I know she really doesn't want to be doing this. But I have to admit, we all take some sadistic pleasure in denying Shayna James the number-one position." April fist-bumped June. "Merry still plans on being at the wedding on Saturday."

"Shayna James and Dusty Greaves are not that important. They are my past. And it seems like the Three

Sisters Ranch is my future."

"You don't have to sound so miserable about it." Penny cleaned up the counter with the wet rag.

"I like what I'm doing," June said. "But I'd be lying if I said I didn't miss the rodeo circuit. I'm not used to all this quiet. It makes me think. And when I think, I get nervous."

"What are you thinking about that makes you so nervous?" Penny asked.

"Life, the universe, everything. I'm wondering if I've peaked. And if I'm like one of those high school football players who'll keep reliving their glory days fifty years down the line. What if the best has already happened to me?"

"Don't talk nonsense," Penny said. "Maybe a chapter in your life is closed. But that doesn't mean the whole book is ending. You just have to find some new excitement. And let me tell you, if I was your age and living with six handsome, virile young cowboys, I wouldn't be sitting at my mama's kitchen table. That's for damn sure."

"Yeah, about that... I might've made a big mistake."

"Oh no, June," April said. "Please tell me you didn't do something reckless."

"Well, by reckless, do you mean like forgetting to tighten Athena's saddle?"

"No, but you haven't been drinking again. Have you?"

June rolled her eyes. But it was a fair question. "I wouldn't mind kicking back with a beer or shot of whiskey, but I know I wouldn't stop with one. There were times these past few weeks that I wanted to drink myself to sleep. Or wanted to drink out of boredom. But I never was a solo drinker. It's no fun to drink alone. So, no, I haven't been drinking." June rubbed her arms, suddenly cold. "But I really wanted to." She tried not to think of the open bottle of wine in the fridge. It probably was flat or sour. But still, it called to her. She drank her seltzer in defiance and poured herself another glass.

"Then what did you do that was so reckless?" April asked.

"I somehow got into a serious relationship, I think."

"What?" April flew up out of her chair and clapped her hands. "I can't believe you didn't tell me. With who?"

"Esteban."

April shrieked. "No way!"

"Who's Esteban?" Penny asked, putting out the leftover meats and cheeses with a hunk of Italian bread.

"He's one of the virile, handsome cowboys June lives with in the bunkhouse. And he's also June's boss," April said.

"I thought that was Nate, and he's married."

"Esteban is Nate's second-in-command. So technically, he's not my boss."

"Supervisor, then," April said. "Why didn't Merry and I get all the details?"

"I have no words," June said with a hand over her heart.

"That's my girl," Penny drawled. "Now tell me why you only think you're in a serious relationship."

"His family hates me. His coworkers hate me. We're keeping it a secret to avoid the drama, but it sucks. He texted me that he's still into me, but I'm not so sure that's the truth."

June hung her head. She was afraid that now Esteban got her to agree to being exclusive, she wasn't as exciting anymore. Maybe, she didn't live up to his fantasy. And that did more than hurt her feelings—it played into her deep-rooted fear that she was nothing if she wasn't barrel racing.

"I'm sure he's just busy," April said. "I don't know a lot about Esteban, but he always seemed really polite and nice."

"Yeah, he is polite and nice."

"Even in bed?" Penny asked.

Most mothers didn't ask questions like that. Then again, most mothers weren't married seven or eight times in the course of their children growing up. June answered honestly. "Yes, he did all the gentlemanly things and still managed to rock my world."

"I'm not getting the problem," Mama said.

"The problem is, he's ghosting her," April said.

"It's not really ghosting. I see him every day. We work together. But he makes sure that we're never alone together. He doesn't make eye contact, and if it looks like we're about to be alone, he walks away. He's pretending there's nothing between us."

"I'm going to go out on a limb here," Penny said.

"Maybe you shouldn't." April winced.

"Nonsense, your sister came here for advice."

"Actually, I came here for lasagna." June ripped off a chunk of bread and dipped it into her mother's leftover sauce. She closed her eyes and hummed in delight. Yeah, that was better than wine.

"I'm assuming you rocked his world as much as he

rocked yours?"

"That was my impression."

"I think he'll come around. You probably threw him for a loop because he thought he had to work for it a little bit more."

"I don't get the whole 'work for it' thing," June said. "We're consenting adults. Why on earth would we need to wait until after the third date or two weeks or whatever society thinks it is? I was horny. He was horny. He told me he'd always had a crush on me, and had followed my rodeo events."

"Oh, isn't that the sweetest thing," Penny said.

"But maybe you're right. Maybe he lost interest because I was too easy."

"Don't jump to conclusions," April warned.

"Or maybe he's feeling guilty about being with me when his family hates me."

"Why on earth would they hate you?" Penny said. "Are they Shayna James fans?"

"I stole the job out from under Esteban's brother, but I didn't mean to. I don't blame them for being mad, but I didn't know."

"You can't control what Emily does and who she gave the job to. For whatever reason, she chose you as the right person for the job," Penny said.

"I wasn't the right person for the job."

"It doesn't matter. Do you want to quit?"

"No. This might not be my forever job, but it's something I'm committed to. I intend to give it my best shot."

"Then they'll come around, though it might not be as quick as you're used to. But the lasagna will help." Penny rapped her knuckle on the aluminum foil top. "Your hard work and your willingness to be part of their team will also help them come around."

"What if they don't?" June said. "What if I am working with six Shayna Jameses?"

"I doubt that's the case. But if it is, you get Emily to watch your back and start looking for another job. You'll know when it's time to move on. But don't let anybody guilt you into stopping what you want to do."

"Thanks, Mama." June felt a little better after talking with them. "I'm still not sure how to win over Esteban's family."

"They'll come around. Just be patient," April said.

"How do I get them to like me?" June said.

"Lasagna always works."

June looked at the seven trays thoughtfully.

ESTEBAN WAS HOPING to catch June after dinner to talk to her, and apologize for being so distant this week. Luis was being a spy and informing his family about everything she did, no matter how small. If Esteban helped her with something, Luis texted it out and the next thing he knew, his mother was reading him the riot act. But he missed her, even if he was having a hard time coming to terms with pursuing his own happiness over his family's unhappiness.

"Have you seen June?" Esteban asked. There were a few hands hanging around in the common area after he'd finished cleaning up with the dishes.

Ringo smirked. "She got into her truck and drove away. Do you think we scared her off?"

"You damn well better not have. Have you guys been up to any shenanigans this week?" Esteban asked casually, but he was feeling anything but casual inside.

"No, man, we've been good."

"You better keep it that way, especially since I'm not going to be around to watch over you tonight and tomorrow." He had the bachelor party tonight and the day off tomorrow.

"Geez, ever since June started, you've been like our babysitter. June's got nothing to fear from us. She can take some good-natured razzing and give back as good as she gets. You don't have to treat her like she's made of glass," Bob said.

"Yeah," Frenchie said. "You should be more worried about getting your ass handed to you tonight and losing your shirt in the poker game."

"What kind of bachelor party doesn't have any strippers?" Bob said. "You can play poker every Saturday night. A man only has a bachelor party once. You have to make it memorable."

"With Cole dealing the cards, I only have to worry about Charlie," Esteban said.

The bachelor party was taking place in the common room of Janice's wellness center. Janice had arranged for a catered tray of snacks and a selection of top-shelf booze to be set up in the area. While she threatened them with death if they smoked inside, no one would care that they took cigars out on the porch in between sets. It would be a nice relaxing night, which appealed to all of them. There had been a lot of drama over the past few months, and this would be a great way to celebrate the end of them, while at the same time, celebrating Donovan and Emily's upcoming wedding.

Because he had to clean up from dinner, Esteban was one of the last people to arrive. However, when Charlie saw him approaching the retreat center, he got out of his car and jogged over to him. "Took you long enough. I was waiting for you."

"Why me?"

"I didn't want to go in there all alone. I was afraid Donovan and I might get into an argument, and I didn't want to ruin this night for him."

"Think of it as just a poker game," Esteban said.

"It's not, though. He's gone out of his way to avoid me ever since I came here. And he's got good reason. But I want him to see that I've changed. Years in prison will do that to a man."

"Emily seems to think that you're worth a second chance. Donovan would do anything for Emily, so you've got that going for you."

"I couldn't think of a more perfect wife for my son. Emily has become like a daughter to me. And because of that, her friends are my friends. Even if they don't know I'm their friend."

"What do you mean?"

"I didn't realize that you and June were involved when I mentioned what had happened to her in the bar the other night."

"We're not really involved," Esteban said, looking around. He hated having to lie about June being his, but it was just until they hired Sam. Then it wouldn't look like June had slept her way into the position and he wouldn't have to beat the shit out of anyone.

"My mistake," Charlie said. "In that case, let me be blunt. I can get June back into the WPRC and free up a job slot for your brother, Sam."

That stopped Esteban in his tracks. "What are you talking about?"

"I dug a little deeper into the situation like you requested."

"I didn't mean for you to go out of your way."

"I would have done it anyway, because of the situation that evolved."

Esteban had the feeling he was getting in over his head. "What happened?"

"I found out that when Emily hired June, she received a phone call from your guy, Sinclair Thompson. He's a PR suit for the Women's Pro Rodeo Circuit."

"Let me guess, Sinclair offered Emily something to fire June."

"How do you know that?" Charlie asked, tilting his head.

"Because he said he'd give Trent free advertising and a WPRC-sponsored barrel-racing trainer for the summer if he didn't hire June."

Charlie nodded. "That makes sense. For Emily it was a gift of a new combine if she told June to take a walk."

"They're spending a lot of money to ruin June's life." Esteban's fists clenched. "I'm assuming Emily told them to fuck off?"

"And then she got vulgar with them."

Esteban smirked.

"But it's not they, it's him. Sinclair Thompson. He's got money to burn and he doesn't use it for good. He even looked into buying up a few of the ranch's debts to put pressure on Emily."

"June would quit before she let that happen."

"I think that was his intention. If he couldn't get Emily to flinch, he could go to June and tell her that she's responsible for her friend being in a bind."

"He's not going to get away with this," Esteban said.

"No, he's not. I'm going to make sure June goes back to the rodeo and your brother gets the job. I just wanted to make sure you're on board with this before I do it."

"Do what?"

"Put a stop to his harassment once and for all."

"Why is he even doing this? What does he have against her?"

"Sinclair Thomas was a busy man in his youth. He's Shayna James's father."

"No shit," Esteban said. "Well, that would explain things."

"He wants his baby girl on top. But it gets even juicier than that. He's also June's father."

"What?" Esteban shook his head. "He can't be. June said her father's in Tallahassee somewhere."

"It's not common knowledge. I doubt even June knows. But I have friends who can find out things that most people think are buried. Sinclair hates Penny Grayson for not leaving her husband for him. He wants to punish June for her mother's sins, while putting the child that he loves better on top. But he went too far when he took away her boyfriend and her career. You think that would be enough. But Penny and June weren't suffering. Penny was thrilled June was home. And June was thriving."

"I'm not sure I'd call it thriving," Esteban said.

"But Sinclair made a mistake when he went after June's horse."

"Athena?" Esteban whirled to head back to the barn to check on her.

Charlie pulled him back. "She's safe. The muscle Sinclair had hired was caught red-handed by Nate who turned him over to the police a few hours ago. The bastard must have had someone watching June's mother's trailer. As soon as June arrived, he headed to the ranch. He hadn't expected Nate and Janice to be…" Charlie cleared his throat. "…in the barn."

Esteban smirked. He should have thought of that spot to meet up with June.

"Anyway, I have a lawyer friend who is negotiating a deal. If the Three Sisters Ranch drops the trespassing charges, the stooge will go on record that Sinclair actively set about the events that got June blackballed from the WPRC."

"Is he credible?"

"He put the roofie in June's drink himself."

The night seemed to go completely still. "He what?"

"Remember I told you that June went to rehab?"

Esteban gave a curt nod.

"She had been set up. Sure, she drank a lot. She always had. This time, though, our stooge slipped her something to turn her drunk up to eleven."

"I'm going to kill him," Esteban said calmly, and started walking back to his car.

Charlie tugged him back. "Don't be an idiot. We need him to turn against Sinclair in order to get June reinstated, especially when Dustin Greaves adds in his two cents."

"What does that asshole have to do with anything?"

"This is where Merry Grayson comes in. She had a showdown with her sister's ex and it was a sight to see. From what I hear, she grabbed him by the balls until he talked."

Esteban smirked. Good.

"Dustin sang like a canary—a soprano canary. He said he was told that he needed to pretend to have an affair with Shayna to generate more publicity for the rodeos. Specifically, soap-opera-level drama. Dustin assumed that June and Shayna were playing their parts, too."

"So he didn't cheat on June," Esteban said.

Charlie shrugged. "He's no angel. But it wasn't his idea to be with Shayna to begin with. But no matter what happens there, Sinclair will be finished in the WPRC and June can get her life back."

"And Dustin." Esteban couldn't believe it. For a moment, he'd had it all and now it was slipping through his fingers. He didn't think June would forget about him on the circuit, but he was pretty sure that a long-distance exclusive relationship wasn't what she was looking for.

"If she wants him, he'll dump Shayna like a sack of horse manure." Charlie looked at him. "But that's neither here nor there. Emily's friend is safe and back where she's supposed to be, and Sam gets the position like he should have had when Emily created the opening. This is what you wanted, right? Sam to be a ranch hand?"

"Yeah," Esteban said. But not at the cost of losing June.

"I thought you'd be happier about this. If you want, I can keep this information quiet and just have a talk with Sinclair about leaving the Three Sisters Ranch out of his plans for punishing Penny Grayson and their daughter."

It had been a great fantasy, thinking he could tame a wild Grayson sister and keep her at his side. But Esteban had to face the facts. He knew June wasn't happy at the Three Sisters Ranch. And while he might have made her bed warmer and they'd connected in a way that would haunt him for the rest of his days, he knew he couldn't take this chance away from her. Her father, a man she didn't even know existed, had tried to destroy her life. June had done nothing wrong. But if Sinclair had never started his machinations with Dustin Greaves, Esteban would never have met June. Not like he had, anyway. He needed to be grateful for the time that they'd had together and not mourn for what could have been.

"Esteban? Are you okay? We really should be getting inside." Charlie took him by the elbow.

"Yeah, you're right." He walked into the retreat center with Charlie and nearly recoiled at the look in Donovan's eyes when he gazed at his father.

"Fathers make mistakes," Charlie said to Esteban in a low voice. "But Sinclair deliberately set out to destroy his child's life. I can't allow that."

"I don't want you to," Esteban said, and then in a louder voice said, "I'm not going easy on you, Donovan. Better get a drink and a cigar now, because you're going down."

Some of the tension broke when Donovan replied, "In your dreams, Esteban."

In his dreams, there was a happily ever after with June. He thought he had the time to make it happen, but it turned out to be as fleeting as the smoke rings from Nate's cigar.

# Chapter Sixteen

I T HADN'T BEEN easy to find out where Esteban's mother lived. June had decided to resort to bribery, so she went back to the bunkhouse and warmed up a tray of lasagna, then gave out samples as a preview of tomorrow's dinner on the pretense of asking for advice on making it better. Eventually, Luis came down for a piece.

After he was finished, she cornered him. "Hey, I want to talk with your family."

"They don't want to talk with you," he said.

"I am not the enemy," she said. "I didn't know that Sam was waiting for the job I stepped into."

"You do now," Luis said, his tone and stance hostile. "Why don't you go back to the rodeo where you belong?"

She wanted to tell him that she didn't belong there anymore, even if they decided to take her back. "My life is here now." June was ready to try a new direction, with Esteban by her side, of course.

"My brother's girl, Anne, is pregnant," Luis blurted out.

*Pregnant?*

"Her parents threw her out. Sam's away on a short-term job, but it's not enough for them to move out of my mom's house and start on their own. Not with a baby coming."

Guilt thrummed through her. June wondered again if she should quit the ranch. She could live rent-free in her mother's house. That way, Esteban wouldn't have to worry about hiding their relationship with his family, and Sam would have a steady job to support his child.

It felt like she was throwing Emily's kindness back in her face, though. But if she waited until after the wedding, June wouldn't have to face her friend until she got back from her honeymoon. It was obvious that Sam needed the job more than she did. She only had herself to worry about. Her bills would get paid somehow. Maybe Cole could take her around with him when he moonlighted on the other farms. If it would stop the pressure Esteban's family was putting on him, it would be worth it. If worse came to worst, she'd sweep up hair for tips as her mother's shampoo wench or something.

"Look, I don't want to cause problems," she said. "It's been a week and you guys have made it clear I'm not welcome. I'll quit and Nate can hire Sam. Just let Emily have her wedding day first, okay?"

Luis shifted uncomfortably. "It's nothing against you. Nothing personal."

"It feels personal," June said, trying to keep the bitterness out of her voice.

No one wanted her. Except Esteban. She held on to that.

"I don't think Emily knew that Sam had been promised the next open position. And I didn't know how much of a problem it would cause here when I took it."

"If you leave, Esteban will be pissed at us."

"That's your problem." June wanted to do this for Esteban and for his brother, Sam. Wasn't this what April had been talking about? Compromising in the relationship. It was so much easier when she had one-night stands. Easier, but not as satisfying. The thought of helping Esteban's family helped her feel a little less hollow inside. "But you're stuck with me until after the wedding. I don't want anything to upset Emily."

"Deal." He stuck out his hand to shake.

"What are we agreeing to?" she asked warily.

"You quit the day after Emily's wedding so Nate can get Sam in there. After that, we'd love to have you back on the crew once other positions open up—if you're not already back on the circuit."

She shook his hand. She'd figure some way to make money—something Sinclair Thompson couldn't touch, and somewhere that allowed her to be outside and around horses.

"How's Dina doing?" June asked.

Luis looked up in surprise. "She's looking forward to her lessons."

Another kick in the chest. But Sinclair couldn't stop her from giving private lessons. "How about I take over a tray of lasagna and let Dina ride Athena? I'll trailer her up and bring her to your mom's house."

"Are you kidding me?" he said. "When?"

"I don't have a free day off until after the wedding, but any time after that."

"She'll flip. She has her own Bad Reputation hat."

June closed her eyes and groaned. "I bet her mother loves that."

"Beatriz does. Mamá, not so much."

"Give me your address." June typed it into her phone. "Can I trust you with a secret?"

"Sure," Luis said.

"Your brother and I are dating."

"Yeah, no shit. What's the secret?" Luis said expectantly.

"That is the secret," June said, deadpan.

"Everyone knows that." He shook his head.

"Why didn't you guys mention it?"

He shrugged. "We figured you wanted to keep it on the down-low."

"So are you guys all right with that? Me sleeping with Esteban?"

"Does anyone else have a chance with you?"

"No," June said.

"Then we don't care."

"Just to be clear, when you say everyone, do you mean…"

"Everyone." Luis put his plate and silverware in the dishwasher. "Thanks for doing this. It means a lot. If you're with my brother for the long haul, this is the right thing to do. I'll work on Mamá. She'll come around, especially when she sees how happy you make Esteban. It'll just take time."

"Patience isn't my strong suit."

"What's the alternative?"

He had a point.

JUNE WAS STARTLED out of a deep sleep when a warm body slid into bed next to her. A hot, wet mouth sucked on her neck while a rough calloused hand caressed her breast.

"That better be you, Esteban," she whispered, even though she had already recognized the feel of his body against hers. He smelled like sweet cigar and whiskey. She was wet even before he reached between her legs.

"We have to be quiet," he whispered in her ear. "I need you tonight. I need you so damned much."

Still half asleep, she spread her legs wide for him as he rubbed her body into a frenzy. Kissing her neck, playing with her breast and rubbing her clit, Esteban was well on the way to making her come.

"The bed is going to make noise." Arching into him, June rubbed her ass against his hard cock. "Although, the thought of getting caught makes me hot."

Flinging the covers back, he scooped her out of bed and carried her into the shower, then turned it on full blast. "This should cover some of the noises I'm going to pull out of you."

"Is that right?" she said before sinking to her knees in front of him. He was as naked as she was.

Moving the bath mat so she was kneeling on that instead of the cold, hard tile, June licked up his cock.

"I'm sorry I woke you," he said, cupping her cheek. "But I couldn't stay away."

"I had to be up in a few hours anyway," she said. "I'll

sleep later. This is too good to miss."

She took him deep in her throat, loving how Esteban hissed and went up on his toes. She needed him, too. Slowly, she bobbed her head up and down his shaft. His head was thrown back and his fingers tangled into her hair.

Esteban whispered her name over and over again, the harsh syllable echoing off the tile. As the bathroom filled with steam, she moaned and sucked hard on him before soothing it with her tongue.

"Mine," he panted.

She loved seeing him like this, slightly out of control and almost feral with desire. He guided her head so she took him deeper. Gladly, she let him fuck her mouth while she kneaded his tight ass. Groaning, he propped his hands on the wall.

"Coming," he warned.

She swallowed as his hips jerked and he bit his wrist to keep quiet. Still, his harsh pleasured grunts satisfied her.

"Your turn."

June had to stifle a shriek when he lifted her hips straight up. His muscles flexed as he settled her legs over his shoulders. Back against the wall, with Esteban's hands cupping her ass, June was pinned, helpless for his mouth to ravage her sensitive parts.

He kissed her pussy like it was her mouth, deep, probing and with skill and enjoyment. Her hips battered against his face as she strained to get off from the sweet and sexy caress.

"More, more," she begged, rubbing against him for relief from the building friction that was making her thighs quiver and her legs shake.

The unexpected pleasure of tonight made her blood sing. He was a talented and inventive lover and she was so happy to have him in her life. It was too soon for her to contemplate the "L" word, but he was closer than any man had ever been.

Terrified that he'd slip and drop her, she whispered, "Put me down."

But before he could, her orgasm shook through her. He slid her down his body to the floor and marched her over to the sink, facing the mirror. He took a condom from behind it and then watched her as he put it on.

"Hold on," he said in a dark, sexy voice. Then he nudged her legs apart and sank deep inside her, locking gazes with her in the mirror.

He fucked her hard and she slammed back to meet him stroke for stroke. Mouth open and silently screaming in pleasure, June loved the feel of him driving into her with passionate disregard for technique. This was primal—the mating of two people who had found each other against all odds.

*Take me. Take me*, she begged him with her eyes and he followed through until she was gasping and clenching around him.

Burying his face in her hair, Esteban came inside her with several hard jerks and then shuddered his release.

They froze there, panting for a moment. He broke away first, disposing of the condom and helping her into the shower that was arctic again. After briskly cleaning themselves off, they stumbled back to bed and under the covers.

"I'll stay here until you guys ride off," he said, cuddling her against his chest.

"They all know about us." She yawned.

"Did you tell them?"

"Nope." June buried her face in his chest.

"Are they giving you any shit?"

"No more than usual."

He stroked her hair and she had almost fallen back asleep when he asked, "Are you happy working as a ranch hand?"

Here was her opening. If she said no, he wouldn't be broadsided when she gave her notice. But she didn't want to lie to him. "I like working with you."

Hell, this thing between them was the only thing that was going right in her life just now. It was important to her. June was sure it would end in tears, but she was willing to put the effort in.

"No matter what happens," he said. "My feelings for you won't change."

June didn't have it in her to comment, but she was smiling as she faded back to sleep.

# Chapter Seventeen

JUNE WAS FEEDING the chickens when Merry called. Looking around to see if the other hands were nearby, she answered it. It would have to be a quick conversation because she didn't want Nate or Esteban to get on her case about being on the phone when she was supposed to be working.

"Hey, are you flying in this weekend on your friend's private plane?" June asked.

"The WPRC is about to call you," Merry whispered fiercely. "Pick up the phone and don't be a smartass." She hung up.

"What the...?" June was staring at her phone in disbelief when it rang again with a number she didn't recognize showing up on the caller ID. "Hello?"

"Miss Grayson, this is Shelby Miller. I'm the CEO of the Women's Professional Rodeo Circuit."

Heeding Merry's warning, June decided to be on her best behavior. "How may I help you, Shelby?"

"It's come to our attention that a former employee of ours, Sinclair Thompson, has overstepped his authority regarding your situation."

"My situation?" *Former employee?*

"Yes, we'd like to have you back for the fall season. We think you'll be a great asset to our team and we're looking forward to seeing you compete."

June went hot. Then cold. She ducked into the barn and sank to sitting position against the wall. "I'm not sure that's in my best interest," she hedged, wondering what this new angle was. Were they going to get her to the final competition and publicly denounce her?

"I understand your reticence. We deeply regret not reviewing Mr. Thompson's actions in greater detail. He's done you a great disservice."

"Ya think?" June said before she could stop herself.

"Should you wish to pursue legal actions, we would be happy to testify against him."

June didn't know about that. But she did know that she needed to give them an answer.

She just didn't know what that was going to be. On the one hand, it played into her plan of giving up the ranch job for Sam. On the other hand, she'd be back on the road, away from Esteban.

"Testify?" June said, stalling.

"The night of the unfortunate incident between you, Mr. Greaves, and Ms. James, it has been discovered that your drink had been doctored. Our sources say that Mr. Thompson arranged for that to happen, in order to pressure you into going to rehab and take you out of the competition."

"You're damned right I'm going to testify." June ripped apart the hay bale she was sitting on in anger. Three months of her life, wasted. Forcing herself to take a deep breath, she said, "I need to review my options and get back to you."

She was going to sue his ass from here to the moon, that son of a bitch. She needed to talk to Merry, pronto.

"Of course. You're welcome back at any time. But in the fall, you'll be starting at the same time as everyone else."

"At any time, you say?" June said, perking up as an idea hit her just as she was about to hang up on the woman. "So, if I was to go to the finals, I could compete in the events there."

"Uh, let me check your point standings."

June heard typing in the background. "Yes, you qualify to attend but you won't win the all-around."

"I don't have to," June said. "I'm still qualified for the barrel-racing championship, right?" Even being out three months, she should still have the ranking to compete.

"That's correct."

"Then I'll see you in Dallas."

She disconnected the call and quickly dialed Merry. "What the actual fuck just happened?"

"I can't even right now. I'll tell you when I see you. But believe me when I say, y'all ain't going to believe this shit."

"He put something in my drink, Merry. I'm going to get him for that."

"He's going to suffer," Merry agreed. "Don't you worry. We'll lawyer up and make him pay for doing that to you."

"I want him to hurt," June said.

"He will. For a long time. But there's more to the story. Get here ASAP and we'll share a bottle of wine and I'll give you all the details."

Wine. She didn't have to stop herself from having it now. It hadn't been her fault she'd blacked out. Still, June had lost her taste for it. "I'll bring the sparkling cider."

"Suit yourself."

Next, June dialed Esteban, but the call went right to voicemail. Pocketing her phone, she took off at a full run to find him. But she ran into Emily first.

"June, what's wrong?" Emily grabbed her shoulders to steady her from falling over.

Wheezing for air, June tried to get a breath. "I'm going to kick Shayna James's ass," she forced out.

Emily rolled her eyes. "What did that bitch do now?"

"WPRC wants me back."

"What? That's wonderful!"

"I'm going to Dallas for the finals. I don't qualify for All-Around Champion, so that's Merry's first-place win. But I'm going to ride against Shayna for Barrel-Racing Champ."

"What changed their minds?"

"They caught Sinclair Thompson at his dirty games."

"It serves him right for sending someone here to hurt Athena."

"Athena?" June gaped.

"Janice and Nate found an intruder in the barn yesterday. He was trespassing and Nate said he'd been hired to steal Athena."

"I've got to see her." June took off at another run and Emily jogged after her until they reached the barn.

After assuring herself that Athena was all right, she

hugged the horse's neck. "Where is the intruder? I'm going to break both his legs."

"Save it for Sinclair. The guy sang like a canary that he was just Sinclair's stooge."

"That's how they got their information," June mused.

"The finals are the day before my wedding," Emily said. "You're still going to make it for the ceremony, right?"

"I wouldn't miss it."

"Then bring me back a championship ring," Emily said. "Or shave Shayna James's head bald. One or the other."

"Deal." June straightened. "I also quit. Give the job to Sam Lopez, Esteban's brother."

"Not you, too!" Emily held her hands over her ears. "Fine, I'll hire Sam."

"Thank you." June gave her a hug. "I've got to go find Esteban."

It took about a half hour, but she was able to track him down in the bunkhouse. He was on the phone when she walked into the common area.

"That's great, Sam. I'll be over tonight to help you move in. I'm glad, too. It was a long time coming, but you don't have anything to worry about. I'll see you later."

"Emily moves fast," June said when he got off the phone. She held a hand to her side. She had a sharp pain from running at top speed. "I tried calling, but I got your voicemail. I'm competing in the finals on Friday."

"I figured. Good luck."

"Hey…" She stepped in close to him. "It's only one event. I can earn a year's salary with that purse. If I do, I'm coming back here. To you. Hell, I'm going to do that even if I don't win. But I need to beat Shayna James in the barrel-racing championship. It's not Merry's fight. It's mine."

"Because of Dustin?" he asked, stroking her cheek.

"Because of everything." June told him about the WPRC phone call.

"Ask your mother about Sinclair, and stay away from him. He's out of a job and could decide to be a more direct threat."

"I'm going to sue his ass off for drugging me, but first I'm going to make sure his plans for Shayna are over. I will win that title and I will tell everyone what he did to me."

"Ask your mother about him," Esteban said again, and hugged her.

"Why? She doesn't know Sinclair."

"I bet you she does. But you both might need a drink for that conversation."

"I can drink," she said. "I mean I always could, but I felt a niggle of doubt. Now, we know it was Sinclair screwing with me all along. I can't wait to shove this win up his ass."

"When are you leaving?"

"Soon. I've got to coordinate with Merry and get some practice time in. I know you can't come out and see me…"

"I'll be watching on TV. We all will be."

"I'll see you the next day at the wedding. We have a date. Don't stand me up."

"I love you, June," he said.

Her knees went weak. "I…"

"I don't need to hear it back. Not now. But I wanted you

to know that."

"I'm coming back," she said.

"I'll be here." He kissed her again. It was sweet and sad, and had the taste of finality to it. When he ended the kiss, she was shaken, but not in a good way.

"This isn't goodbye," she told him.

"It better not be."

If it had been anyone else other than Shayna James that she was riding against, June would have said fuck it and taken Esteban to bed.

"I have to do this," she said.

"I know. Go kick ass."

Being reinstated and ready to compete didn't feel the same anymore. Sure, she was excited but everything had changed. Was this what love did to a person?

If she was smart, she'd run and not look back.

June kissed Esteban fiercely. Being smart was overrated.

# Chapter Eighteen

THE NIGHT BEFORE Emily's wedding, Esteban was at his mother's house with the rest of his family, watching the WPRC finals. Beatriz had popped several bowls of popcorn. His brothers were front and center on the couch with Dina between them. All three were watching the television like they were afraid to blink.

Esteban paced around the small living room until Beatriz grabbed him by the shoulders and forced him into a chair.

"You're making me nuts," she said.

His mother and Anne were in the kitchen cooking enough enchiladas to feed an army. But even the delicious smell coming from the oven wasn't enough to distract him. He had already lost June. He knew that in his heart. She would still visit Last Stand and maybe she'd want to renew their affair, but she wouldn't stay. He wanted to punch holes in the walls in frustration, but instead he just worked himself and his crew harder.

"Anything new with Cliff?" Esteban asked. He almost hoped so. It would feel good to beat the hell out of him again.

"He's still pissed at you."

"The feeling is mutual."

"But he voluntarily went into a detox clinic. I think he did it more for her than me," Beatriz said quietly.

She probably didn't have to lower her voice because Dina was too engrossed in the opening sequences of the rodeo to care.

"Have you spoken to her today?" Beatriz asked.

"Yeah, I wished her good luck."

"You really want her to win, huh?"

Esteban couldn't care less. He wanted her back home. He wanted proof that she hadn't changed her mind on their crazy adventure.

"Is she going to keep her clothes on this time?" his mother said, wiping her hands on a dish towel as she came out of the kitchen and sat next to him.

"Mamá," Esteban chided.

"There she is," Dina said, pointing.

Sure enough, June was carrying the American flag as she rode into the arena on Athena, whose mane was braided with beads and little bells. June wore a tight pink blouse and jeans, as well as her Bad Reputation Stetson. Merry came out next with the flag of Texas and then Shayna James, who carried the WPRC flag.

"Please stand for the national anthem," the announcer said.

Dina popped up from her seat and placed a hand over her heart as she warbled out the words.

Beatriz filmed it on her camera.

"Are Sam and Luis doing well at their jobs?" his mother

asked.

"Yeah, so far, so good."

Anne came out carrying a tray of something that smelled garlicky and delicious, but it was not enchiladas. "June brought this over for us to enjoy. It's her mother's home-made lasagna."

Sam and Luis scurried out of the couch to grab plates.

"Wasn't that nice of her, Mamá?" Beatriz said.

His mother sniffed. "She couldn't make it herself?"

"It's so good," Luis said, with his mouth full.

"Our first rider tonight is bottom seed June Grayson," the announcer said.

"June's been MIA for most of this season," the other em-cee of the program added.

"She's a local favorite, though, that's for sure."

"Not everyone is a fan." The camera did a close-up of Shayna James. Esteban hadn't realized how much Shayna hated June until he saw Shayna's expression.

"That's the face of pure evil," Beatriz said, crossing herself.

"You can't blame Shayna for being mad," the announcer said. "June kissed her fiancé."

"What?" Luis said.

They ran the video clip of the interview with Dustin and Shayna—the one where June came up from behind the couple and pulled Dustin in for a kiss. Esteban's eyes narrowed. "It's a publicity stunt," he said between his teeth.

"Sure, it is," Sam said. But it would have sounded more sincere if he hadn't had tomato sauce all over his chin.

The camera came back to June approaching the start. Athena was dancing sideways, ready to run.

"And here we go…" the announcer said.

Athena shot out of the start and went left, then circled tight around the first barrel, digging in low and tight. They sped toward the next barrel and rode the rest of the cloverleaf pattern cleanly. When they headed for home, Athena's legs were a blur. Their time clocked in at 17:17 seconds.

"Not her best time," Luis muttered.

Merry clocked in at 17:47. Three more riders couldn't beat Merry's time. Then it was Shayna's turn.

"I hope she gets thrown," Beatriz spat.

"I don't care what she does as long as she doesn't win," Luis said.

Shayna came around the first barrel fast and technically perfect. She gained speed on the second barrel.

"She's going to do it," Sam said.

"Shut up," Esteban said.

It looked like Sam was right, though. Then a miracle happened. On the third turn, Shayna's horse shouldered the barrel and went down. Esteban shot to his feet. Shayna's time was 14:99, but with the five-second penalty, it knocked her down to third place.

"She did it! She did it!" Dina cried.

"There are still more riders," Esteban said. But in his heart, he knew June had won.

At the end of the finals, June had taken first place in barrel racing. She and Merry finished in second place in team roping. Shayna took first place in breakaway roping. And Merry won the all-around.

Esteban was exhausted, as if he'd been the one competing. The winners' ceremony was quick with the judges presenting the top three in each event with a sash. The first-place winner also received a ring and bouquet of roses. They also got a fat check, but that wasn't shown in the ceremony.

"We have a special presenter for the barrel-racing winners... Ladies and gentlemen, please welcome Men's All-Around Champion, Dustin Greaves."

"That's a good-looking man," his mother said.

"Mamá," Esteban chided.

"She's not wrong," Beatriz added.

Dustin put the sash on Shayna and attempted to kiss her, but she turned her face away and he got her cheek.

"That's cold," Sam said.

Merry accepted her second-place sash. Dustin didn't try to kiss her, and reflexively covered his balls with his hand until he was a safe distance away.

Esteban's fists clenched when Dustin approached June. He gave her the sash and flowers and then sank down on one knee and offered her the ring.

"Wait," the announcer said. "Is that the first-place ring or is he proposing?"

It got really quiet in the Lopez house.

June took the bouquet and buried her nose in it.

A cold panic crept up Esteban's spine.

Then, June tossed the bouquet over her shoulder...and dropped Dustin with a roundhouse punch.

"I guess that's a no," the other announcer said.

Esteban found he could breathe again.

And then they cut to a commercial.

# Chapter Nineteen

J une and Merry bustled into the church at the very last minute. April chewed them out, but Emily just hugged them both.

"Congratulations," she said, and then pushed them out to the church. "Walk slowly."

Kelly and Janice were already up at the altar standing across from their husbands. Merry walked out first and was met by one of Emily's Peace Corps friends. They walked to the end of the aisle and then separated.

Esteban was waiting for June when she came out. He paused to kiss her on the mouth, and it sent a thrill down to her toes. They walked hand in hand down the aisle.

"Get used to it," he said. "It's good practice for when we do this."

"Dream on," she whispered.

"I will."

He kissed her again at the end of the altar.

It had been a crazy week. The nightmare with Sinclair was over, except it wasn't. He was her freaking father. But worse than that, Shayna James was her half-sister. June couldn't wait to tell her and watch her face pucker like a unicorn's anus. Normally, June would serve that tea up on social media. But June didn't want to claim either one of them publicly.

Her mother went for the shotgun when she found out what her former lover had done. After much convincing and a lot of crying, Penny decided to let the courts handle it. Charlie's lawyer was looking at a large cash settlement. June was going to give it all to her mother so she could retire and finally give her feet and back a rest.

June was looking forward to starting up on the circuit again in the fall. She had one more season in her and then she was going to take Trent up on his offer to have her teach barrel racing at his school. Merry wasn't as enthused about the new season, but that's because the WPRC had a new event: bronc riding. And they were expecting Merry to be a strong competitor. She and June were going to have to start training next month.

When the wedding march started, June turned to look at Emily. Her friend was radiant, and her smile was so bright, it looked as if she might break out in tears of joy. June shot a look at Donovan, whose eyes went misty when he looked at his bride. Maybe marriage wouldn't be so bad if she had someone who looked at her the way Donovan was looking at Emily. June turned her head and scanned the room. Or the way Trent looked at Kelly. Or Nate, smiling at Janice. Or Cole, who couldn't take his eyes off of April. Or Esteban...

Esteban wasn't watching Emily's slow walk up the aisle, and he wasn't paying attention to Donovan. Instead, Esteban was staring at her with the same emotion she saw on the faces of all of the other people who were in love.

"I love you," he mouthed.

Lightning struck. The earth moved and tears pricked the corners of her eyes.

"I love you too," she said.

## The End

Want more? Check out April and Cole's story in
*A Cowboy for April*!

Join Tule Publishing's newsletter for more great reads and weekly deals!

If you enjoyed *A Cowboy for June,*
you'll love the next book in the…

## Three Sisters Ranch series

Book 1: *The Cowboy's Daughter*

Book 2: *The Cowboy's Hunt*

Book 3: *The Cowboy's Heart*

Book 4: *A Cowboy for April*

Book 5: *A Cowboy for June*

Book 6: *A Cowboy for Merry*
*Coming November 2021*

*Available now at your favorite online retailer!*

# About the Author

USA Today bestselling author, Jamie K. Schmidt, writes erotic contemporary love stories and paranormal romances. Her steamy, romantic comedy, Life's a Beach, reached #65 on USA Today, #2 on Barnes & Noble and #9 on Amazon and iBooks. Her Club Inferno series from Random House's Loveswept line has hit both the Amazon and Barnes & Noble top one hundred lists. The first book in the series, Heat, put her on the USA Today bestseller list for the first time, and is a #1 Amazon bestseller. Her book Stud is a 2018 Romance Writers of America Rita® Finalist in Erotica. Her dragon paranormal romance series has been called "fun and quirky" and "endearing." Partnered with New York Times bestselling author and former porn actress, Jenna Jameson, Jamie's hardcover debut, SPICE, continues Jenna's FATE trilogy.

Thank you for reading

# A Cowboy for June

If you enjoyed this book, you can find more from all our great authors at TulePublishing.com, or from your favorite online retailer.

TULE
PUBLISHING

Printed in Great Britain
by Amazon